A Different Ending

Amanda Burke Jaworski

Copyright © 2020 by Amanda Burke Jaworski

This is a work of fiction. Names, characters, places, and incidents either are the product of the author's imagination or are used fictitiously. Any resemblance to actual persons, living or dead, events, or locales is entirely coincidental.

All rights reserved. No part of this book may be reproduced or used in any manner without written permission of the copyright owner except for the use of quotations in a book review.

First Edition

ISBN 978-0-578-76617-1

Published by Amanda Burke Jaworski

amandabjaworski@gmail.com

Mom,

Thank you for going above and beyond every day for me. Fifty-one years was not enough time for you and twenty-seven years was not enough time with you. This world is too quiet without you. Forever missing and loving you.

Gram and Poppy,

Thank you for your love and support, but most of all thank you for just being the best grandparents around.

A special thanks to my children because they are my motivation to try harder and harder every day. Alexa Rain and Joseph Gannon deserve nothing but the best.

Also, I am thankful for my family and their support during the time I spent on this project,

Joseph, my sister, and my dad.

Entry #72

In a perfect world, two people fall in love and live happily ever after, right? Hardly. Too bad there's no such thing as perfect – I mean, in a technical sense we create our own definitions for that word, but in society, "perfection" doesn't exist. My New Year's resolution should have been to move on in life or back; either one would have been adequate. Not me, though – my resolution was to buy a stupid notebook a while ago, so I can try to write more. I don't take criticism very well, and that makes venting to a piece of paper a safer option. My attitude blows, and coincidentally the outcome is rarely ever positive. As miserable as I am, there is one common factor for all of the mayhem: my loser boyfriend, Tyler. I have this half-assed boyfriend, who lives with me in this half-assed apartment, who never pays his half of any bills – all of which are not half-truths, but 110% true! Why haven't I left him yet? That answer is fairly simple: I am just as stupid as he is, and I'm too codependent. I can't stand him, but it is better than being alone all of the time. Even if Ty isn't the nicest... However, there is someone else who I'd much rather be with. That's a whole other story, a rather long, complicated tale. I guess I have always been codependent in a way, and that is ~~never~~ NEVER a good trait. At this point, I'm not sure if I have always been this way, always needing another person around, or if this is something that started after all of the things I have been through. I suppose I could have made better resolutions as I am writing all of this, but whatever. By now, it shouldn't be hard for you to determine that I am the definition to the phrase "hot mess". Back to my current ~~life~~ mess – besides it being almost 3 in the morning, I have to be at work at 8 A.M., which means I have to be awake, ready and out the door by 7:20. Thanks for lending a listening ear... Well, page – it's late, but I'm not too sure who to blame... this notebook or this pen? Or my thoughts?

Truly,

The Hot Mess Express

CHAPTER 1

Six o'clock in the morning seems like a great time to be annoyed, right? Of course the "Boyfriend of the Year" isn't in bed, which means one of two things: he never came home in the first place, or he passed out in the living room drunk like always or perhaps even high. It's almost like I'm living with a stranger. A stranger who needs to get back on his medication, considering how quick he snaps at people. The thought of Tyler and I being together for a few years isn't surprising. The surprising part of this matter is how quickly our relationship took a turn for the worst. Our life together started off like a fairy tale, but at this point it's a nightmare. Granted, I went in knowing Tyler always had a different side to him, I just never imagined that I had much to worry about. Since I met him, he always treated me like a princess, and I was able to trust him. At this point, it's a full-out war. Our home is saturated in violence with no visible no solution. If I was able to tell people about these spectacles of rage, I'm certain they'd agree that it has the power to be classified as a war. I wonder if he acted this way with the other girls before me. Tyler always had girls waiting on him, for whatever reason, and to my surprise he didn't give them any attention after we got together. I mean, he's attractive – green eyes, blonde hair, average height, slim build. What I use to think was charming is now clearly his manipulation, and that's how I think he wins these girls over, like myself.

Stumbling into the living room, I notice an empty couch. *Go figure!* Waking up just to get angry is never fun. However, I barely slept last night. Maybe my sadness depleted the sleep sector of my brain. As I walk over to my mirror, I remember that I never laid my clothes out before I went to bed last night. I'm hitting strike two, only ten minutes after opening my eyes. I hate digging through my drawers this early; at least what I threw on has no wrinkles. That's a plus.

Same routine every morning: find my phone, turn my alarm off, get dressed, check to see if Tyler came home, put my hair up, apply some eyeliner and mascara, grab an unhealthy lunch, light a cigarette, then off to work I go. The half-hour walk to work seems like it takes forever, and add on the frustration and stress of Tyler with his famous disappearing act and I am pretty much over this day already.

Three times I called, but still no answer. Hmmm, how should I start this text today?

As soon as I take my gloves off, I stick them in my pocket and begin to type like my life depends on it.

"Trust you...except you don't come home all night and refuse to tell me where you are? Please tell me how the hell you imagine your name and trust to be in the same sentence? GO SCREW YOURSELF!!!" Send...

That will surely get his blood to boil. Who knows if he will actually answer me. Routinely, I walk into work, butt my cigarette, clock in and sneak my cell phone into my pocket, get to my desk and grab my notebook and pen. I then check the list of notes on my desk. I learned to mentally organize my tasks for the day, this way I can manage my time more wisely. Same old tasks: call this doctor, fill envelopes with these orders, send them to that office, copy that census, drop it off at the nurses stations, all while remembering to have extra copies for the other staff. I can't forget logging the employee hours into the system for payroll.

"Good morning, Aliza. How are you today?" Helen the office manager greets me.

Should I tell her the truth, or could that possibly result in a write-up for extreme use of foul language, in addition to demonstrating psychotic behavior?

"Oh you know, just waking up. I'll let you know the answer to that question in a little while… it's too early to tell." I force a chuckle. "Anything good going on today, or the same old crap?" Here I am, pretending like I care.

"Besides Corporate coming in, nope… nothing."

"Oh no, I totally forgot my nametag. Of course. It never fails!"

With a look of disapproval and maybe even a tad bit of pity, Helen runs into her office and comes back out with a new nametag in less than five minutes. Some people say she's a mega bitch and although that does hold a lot of truth, she is always very nice to me. I like her, I always did. People also think she is snooty, simply due to her seriousness at work. That's the thing, though – Helen is all about work when she is here and I admire that quality, a lot. She grew on me over the years, seeing as my desk is right outside of her office. I guess we are work neighbors.

"Thank you, Helen. It's just one of those mornings," I say with a faint smile.

"Well, you better turn 'one of those mornings' into something productive, or it's going to be one of those days, too. We need all employees on deck today," she says in a serious tone.

"Don't worry, I'm ready to deal with them," I declare.

As Helen walks away, the phone rings.

"Coal County Senior Living, Aliza speaking." My business voice is way different than my normal voice. Call after call, corporate employees are watching my every move as they walk in and out, mild chaos ensuing due to some aides forgetting to fill gaps in their care sheets from last week and just like that, its lunchtime. I don't know why I'm so relieved. All I'm going to do is check my phone and get mad for various reasons. Those various reasons being, Tyler either decided to text me back with a nasty reply, or he didn't care to text back at all. To no surprise, he hasn't said a word. Naturally that prompts me to call him, but his phone is off... well, I tried.

Whatever. I guess I'll shoot Nolan a text. Nolan and I are close friends. We've been friends for a while. We met through mutual friends and always clicked. *"Hey, are ya busy later or no?"*

Luckily, he usually replies within ten to thirty minutes. To my surprise, not even a whole ten minutes later, he answers me back. That might be a world record.

"Nope, I need a cigarette and can't find my ID. You home?"

I wish I was home, especially after the aggravation caused by my part-time boyfriend, but work is a minor distraction.

"I'll be home in like three hours, stop over. Want me to grab ya a pack on my way home?"

"If you can. I will give you the money when I get there."

"K, cya later."

I put my phone in my pocket and walk into the hallway. Time is really dragging for the second half of the day. I got through all of my work before lunch, too. As a result, I'll have to find something to do, or just pretend that I'm busy. Contemplating my options, I decide to just pretend that I'm busy. A soul-sucking leech of a person can take a lot out of someone; plus, I can use the remainder of the day to relax. Not to mention, the phone never stops ringing. That makes me look like I'm busy. Not even one minute later, here comes one of the corporate ladies walking my way.

"Hi, how are you today?" I ask in my best business voice.

"Good. Are you a full-time or part-time receptionist here?" she asks.

"Full-time. I work Monday through Friday, from 8:00 until 4:00. Is there something that I can help you with?"

While arranging papers on her clipboard, she looks up. I can see a test question about to come out of her mouth.

"If a person were to call and ask for a resident's phone number, how would you handle this call?"

Oh, this is a good one and I am, in fact, eager to answer it. My answer is usually on target. I always give a statement that plays it safe. Rule of thumb, in case you're stuck, vague is the way to go, especially if you are unsure of the answer. I'm not trying to brag by saying I have the winning statement or anything. I turn completely towards her, in order to make eye contact.

"In a very polite manner, I would tell them that I will connect them with the nurse's station responsible for that resident's hallway. The nurse can let them speak with their requested party. I would never give a resident's private number to anyone over the phone. The resident and their nurses can determine who they want to give their room number to."

"Very good," she applauds me on my answer in an unenthusiastic, monotone way.

Flipping pages over on her clipboard, she starts up again. "Also, it is the law for all employees to have access to a resident's information, with the responsibility of honoring HIPAA. Bearing in mind the location of your position on the other side of the facility's locked doors, you are educated on changes, especially those who are a flight risk. How are you able to identify those residents, and where is the information stored? In addition to the changes, how often are you updated on specific changes for every resident?"

Slowly opening the second drawer of my desk, I point to the folders stored there.

"This is where I keep my residents' information. Each colored folder represents a hallway. All of our residents' family information, addresses, and other similar data is kept in the business office, all of which I have access to. Their diagnosis and other changes I can view, simply by pulling their copied documents out. We make sure these documents don't provide any more information besides risk warnings… flight risk, diets, room number, anything that isn't sensitive data.

"When needing additional information, I'm able to obtain that through the business office. The business office key is one of the three keys you see hanging from my keyring. We keep our flight risk residents' pictures in this binder to the right of my desk. You can see that we put their first name and room number only under their pictures. I'm updated on changes when the morning meeting and care plans are over," I finish with a smile.

I can tell that she's pleased with my answers. I'm praying this trivia game is over, since I felt my phone vibrate in my pocket a few seconds ago. I'm dying to check my messages, ASAP.

Once she stops writing, she looks up and says, "Clearly you know the way things need to be done. It seems most employees are knowledgeable when it comes to the rules and procedures. Ideally, staff need to be on a proficient level when it comes to all matters; provisional or long-term."

Thank God that went well! Now that she is gone, I need to see if someone can cover the phone. Plus, I aced that pop quiz, resulting in a much-deserved break.

"HELENNN! Hey, can you take watch over the phone? I'm running to the bathroom really quick!"

"Guess I have no choice, huh?"

"Thank you, I'll be back in a minute," I yell while keying in the hallway door code.

While I'm dreading the text that came in, I'm also a glutton for punishment. I can't help but want to read it, too. Once I shut and lock the door, I put the toilet cover down, only to be disappointed... not like I didn't expect this. What do you know, this loser FINALLY decided to text me back. It only took him half the friggin' day to respond!

"Shut the fuck up! If you weren't constantly aggravating me when I'm out, I wouldn't keep going out."

The second I process those words, I see red! I am so sick of being blamed for his immature, inexcusable shit that he does every week.

"Okay, I forgot everything is my fault… normal, considerate boyfriends don't stay out all night without telling their gf where they are or who they are with!"

"All you want to do is argue. Give it up already."

At this point, my hands are shaking and I need a cigarette. Not to mention, I have to get back to my desk. I definitely have been gone for at least ten minutes. There is no reason for him to be mad at me – all I did was ask him why he never came home last night. I have every right to be mad and question him. He never tells me the truth, and I've had suspicions that he cheated on me in the past. Of course, I was right. Considering that not long after that feeling, I caught him trying to cheat. 'Trying to cheat' means he was on social media slick-talking other women. Tyler was caught long before he had the chance. What does he expect from me?! I quickly sit down at my desk and let Helen know that I'm back. I don't even have two hours left. Thank the high heavens!

I quickly get up, leaning into Helen's office. "Hey, did Corporate leave already?" I asked.

"I'm not positive. If anything, they're in the conference room. I think we're in the clear for the most part, though. How did it go when she was questioning you?" she asks, without taking her eyes off the billing program.

"It actually went really well, I think. She seemed pleased with my answers. Oddly enough, her questions were a piece of cake. Today seemed like it went better than any other visit from them, but either way, we'll find out on Monday."

"Typical Corporate fashion, come in on a Friday and let us spend all weekend worrying," she laughs.

Not wanting to appear rude, I laugh with her and act as if I was going to worry in the first place. The reality is though, the second I clock out, I won't think about work until I clock in on Monday. Now that I'm in the clear, it looks like I can reply to this inconsiderate asshole. I am so pissed off that he is acting this way. But it's his normal way of acting when he knows he is in the wrong.

CHAPTER 2

"I can't imagine how you would act if I pulled this shit all the time? Too bad I can't, considering I am the only one who pays the bills in this place! Maybe you should worry less about partying with a bunch of scumbags and start worrying more about getting a job. I refuse to pay bills for us both. I sent you how many *wanted listings the other day? Did you even inquire about any of them?"*

"Don't worry about it, bitch. When I find the job I want, I'll take it! Until then, leave me the fuck alone."

Leave him alone? Does he not see that I do everything all of the time? He never meets me halfway, ever. I am literally going to send one more text, but then I have to put my phone away. He is not worth getting myself upset the way he upset me this morning when I noticed he wasn't home.

"How about this – Stay the hell away from MY apartment that I pay for! Get a job, then you can come back home. Until then, go do whatever it is you do with those whores and trash you talk to! I am sick of you thinking you can do what you want, as if you don't have any responsibilities. I hate to break it to you, but we have our own place and

bills… all of which I handle, since you don't ever plan on growing up!"

The second I put the cell phone in my pocket, the work phone rang. "Coal County Senior Living, Aliza speaking… Okay, let me page Admissions for you."

After putting the woman on hold, I announce the call over the loud speaker. I use to be embarrassed to do that; I have no idea why, either. Now it's second nature to me.

"Who is it? What do they want?" Helen yelled in.

"Some Ellen Lowes…she wants to talk with Melissa about a private room opening. Do you want to take the call?"

"I have to. Melissa is in with Corporate now, anyway. I have no idea how long she'll be."

"I left the lady holding on line two."

Helen nodded, mouthed "thank you" and smiled. She then answered the phone. This day really couldn't have gone any slower. I am so sick of being upset by someone who doesn't care about anyone's feelings, with the exception of his own. Stupid is as stupid does. Using my head is a trait that needs serious improvement for the sole reason that dropping him like a bad habit needs to happen. After straightening up my desk for the weekend part-timer, I bundle up, wave goodbye to Helen, who is still on the phone, clock out and start my walk home. The weather is extremely cold, and the sucky part about winter is the fact that it gets dark very early. When I leave for work in the morning, it is dark. When I leave work to go home, it is almost dark. I always find myself in a lose-lose situation. Two blocks from my apartment is a Sheetz convenience store; at least it is warm in there. If it wasn't for me being desperate for warmth, I would have forgotten to grab Nolan's cigarettes. It's common sense that fishing out my ID and money with gloves on is impossible, but I'm so cold that I make it work.

The second I walk into my house, I hang up my coat, kick my shoes off and light a cigarette. When it is under thirty degrees outside, you learn to wait and smoke when you get home. Five minutes later, Nolan walks in. He throws his coat on the floor and walks into the kitchen. We're past the stage in our friendship where you need to greet each other. We usually go right for one another's fridge before anything is even spoken aloud.

"Here's the money. Thanks for grabbing them. I have no idea what I did with my ID," he says.

"Did you even look for it or not really?'

After exhaling some smoke, he claims he looked everywhere, but I'm sure if I went over to his place I could find it. What would seem like an awkward silence to others ensues, then I notice him out the corner of my eye just staring at me. When I catch him all spaced out and gawking at me, I love it in a weird, uncomfortable way… I can't complain, but I have to say something and break the monotony.

"Tyler didn't come home last night… again…" I tell him.

"What's this, his weekly thing now?"

"Basically, he won't tell me where he is or what he is doing and if I ask, he says I'm a psycho. It just turns into a huge fight. I'm so over it."

"Do what he does, then. Go out and don't tell him anything," he says with a smirk.

It's a smirk that I have come to know as the "Nolan has something up his sleeve" look. A smirk that I always enjoy, due to the fact that whatever he has up his sleeve always involves me. I'll play dumb, like I know how. I can't make it seem like I am too into him, if that is even possible to dull down.

"Sure, let me call my friends that I don't have, so I can plan something. That sounds like a *great* idea. Why thank you so much for that… just one problem, I barely even know anyone anymore. Clearly, that won't suffice," I say in a sarcastic tone.

Shaking his head, he comes over to me, gives me half of his lit cigarette and says, "I'm not doing shit this weekend, so let's hang out. There's most likely something going on – I'll ask around, or we can plan something by ourselves."

There is something about this angle, me sitting on the couch, while he is standing over me. I mean, from all angles he looks great, but this one I'm pretty much drooling over.

"I guess we can figure something out, if you don't forget about me."

"Stop playing."

I don't know about him, but I'm starving. I walk into the kitchen and ask him if he wants to stay and eat. I have no idea why I even ask, he always says yes. This right here is what I want. Being able to come home from work, relax with someone, talk, watch television, sit in silence, eat dinner. Not a single argument or anything; it's just simple. I would kill for this, exactly. One huge problem with this, though – Nolan is just a friend, and I'm dating a total jerk. I finally decide on making chicken Alfredo, which he always seems to like.

"Nol, buddy…can you do me a favor and grab me milk, heavy cream, cheese and some spices, while I cook the chicken?"

Without a single complaint, he comes in and gets everything I asked for and just stands against the refrigerator… staring like usual. I can only act like I don't notice him for so long before I have to break the silence again. Turning around, I look at him and for a couple seconds I don't say a word. I can't… now, I'm doing what he does best, staring. Unlike me, he doesn't hide that he notices me doing it, he just smirks that stupid smirk that I love.

"The noodles are just about done. I have to drain them, make the sauce and it will all be ready in fifteen minutes. Sound good?"

"Whatever you say, Betty Crocker."

"Good one, except not really," I say, laughing.

Once everything is ready, I throw it on plates and we make our way into the living room to eat. I hate to say it, but my kitchen table is the most unstable thing in this house, next to my relationship. This used to be my mother's table, until she bought a new one around the time I was looking for apartments. Over time, the screws that secured the legs had fallen out. However, being free, it was perfect and I assumed Tyler could fix it. Undoubtedly, all of my money is spent on bills and food, and as a result I can't afford a new table right now. The last thing I'm worried about is a damn piece of furniture, though. I need a *car*!

When I finally sit down, I look over and he is downing the alfredo. I can cook a mean dinner, despite what anyone else thinks. We eat in silence, which is fine since I was starving and evidently he was too. Unless he is at his parents' house or mine, he doesn't usually make dinner. He's your typical bachelor, living in the moment.

"What do you want to do tomorrow?" he catches me off guard.

"You know I don't care, as long as it's fun.," I say, shrugging my shoulders.

"Yeah right, he's your boo."

"Next time I'll remember your comment, when you lose your ID and need cigarettes".

"What? I'm just saying… you guys fight today and then next week it will be all fine like it always is," he says, knowing he's right.

I wish he knew how much I really hate that man. Part of me feels bad to leave Tyler because I am too codependent and I don't want to be alone, even though I'm alone a lot as it is. The other part of me doesn't leave him because I'm just so used to him. Neither of those reasons are any good and I totally get that, but hey, I'm a little messed up. We all are. At times like this I want to just come straight out and tell Nolan that I want to be with him and I would leave Tyler's sorry ass in seconds if I had the opportunity. I wonder if I will *ever* have that opportunity.

"It isn't going to stay like this for long. I'm almost at the end point with his selfish ass. You'll see."

As he lights another cigarette, he looks at the TV, then back at me and says, "I guess, I'll see, huh?"

He hands me the cigarette he just lit, then gets himself one. I take both of our dishes out to the kitchen, put them in the sink and as I am walking into the living room, the front door opens and there is Mr. Unemployed himself. Like always, he's in the same clothes he had been wearing two days ago. He shuts the door, walks in, gets a drink, says "hey" to Nolan, then looks at me in a way that basically says he caught me. Too bad – he didn't catch anybody doing anything. God, I hate him so much!

"Cold out there?" Nolan asks Tyler, as if he wasn't just out there.

"Yep. I'm going to smoke this bowl then hop in the shower, I need some sleep. What're you up to?"

"Nothing much, bro. Just stopped over to see what you guys were up to." He plays it off like he came to see us both.

Tyler isn't an idiot, although he is pretty friggin' stupid. He's always bitching that everyone can tell that Nolan and I have feelings for each other and he is sick of coming home and catching him at our house. First of all, this isn't "our" apartment. It is MY apartment, since I pay the bills. Second of all, he needs to let the past go! Nolan and I haven't messed around in years and he knows that, but he will try anything to make me look bad. At this point I am already annoyed, once again.

"I don't know about you guys, but I'm exhausted. I couldn't sleep last night, and after the day I had, I am crashing early," I say more to Nolan than Tyler.

"I hear that. I'll see you guys later, text me or something."

As Tyler's walking into the bathroom to take a shower, he waves bye to Nolan and of course, I go right into the bedroom and shut the door. He really needs to either leave or stay on the couch. I do not want him near me; who knows what – or who – he did last night. I shouldn't be keeping this journal because I'm sure he will read it, but I just don't care. I need to write.

Entry #73

Just another day, annoyed. Tyler finally came home, and I can't wait until he leaves. I'm almost positive Nolan hates when he comes here, too, but he won't say anything, he never does. Tyler has better things and people to worry about, apparently. He hates when Nolan is here when he isn't home. I have no idea who he thinks he is, though giving me a look when he walked in. If Tyler was home and was a decent person, then I wouldn't have to always have Nolan around. It gets lonely here when I'm always mad and literally home by myself on the daily.

Ty won't admit it, but he is really jealous and it shows. He wasn't always an asshole like this. At one point he treated me respectfully, before this whole dating thing. I have no idea why he turned into such an evil person.

We started dating when we were younger, but it wasn't ever serious and it never lasted. We broke up frequently, over stupid teenage drama. In between those break-ups, I would always find myself hanging out with him, though, and we ultimately became inseparable. However, Ty didn't go to my school, which I oddly never complained about.

There is a long history between Tyler and myself. Ty used to be nice. I want to say the drugs changed him. He isn't on anything crazy, I don't think... but he does drink, smoke and take pills on the regular. All of that is what seemed to really change him. I'm no angel, I smoke pot but I was never interested in drugs like that. Nolan nor Ally mess with drugs like that. None of us needed to be on something to enjoy ourselves. Not for nothing, since I was ~~14~~ 15, I've had a major crush on Nolan. It is a super lame story, but it is kind of funny. During the winter that year, we had a snowstorm, and Nolan and his friend Chris were out snowboarding and snowballing at a hill in our neighborhood. Undeniably, I love the snow, so my sister Alora and I were over there, as well. I'd snowboard, while she would just come to hang out.

Anyways, the four of us hung out in the snow all night. We had an awesome igloo and even though I was whitewashed twice, we had a lot of fun, and I couldn't take my eyes off him. Mind you, I had snow pants on, layers of clothes, my hair was a mess, no make-up... I was a disaster!

Yours Truly,

Inquiring Time Traveler

As I hide my new best friend away, my journal, I see the bedroom door crack open. I dread him even coming near me. He walks in, puts his cigarettes on the nightstand and pulls the blankets over his body. Please excuse me while I go vomit, due to this close encounter. Dramatics are a strong suit of mine.

"What are you doing?" I ask him, while looking for my lighter.

"I'm not allowed to sleep in my own bed? Should I ask your permission first? Yeah-fucking-right."

If I have any luck in the world, one day he will not come home at all. I light my cigarette, take my pillow and walk into the living room. If he won't sleep on the couch, I sure as hell will!

CHAPTER 3

AGH! The living room is insanely bright in the morning, I have no idea what time it is and I can't stand the light. Sitting up, I see Tyler walking through the apartment searching for something. I can't imagine what he is looking for, as he possesses nothing of value and I have a lighter right on the table. He looks to be in a hurry, too.

"What are you looking for?" I ask, curiosity getting the best of me.

He looks up, with such anger in his eyes and his lips tightly shut. "I lost twenty dollars somewhere in the house and I need it, now. I'm out of weed and I'm pissed off."

"How did you get money in the first place?"

"Does everything have to be a problem with you?" he snaps.

I have no idea why I even talk to him. "No, all I did was ask a question, my God… Why do you have to be such a dick about everything?"

Now he's mad, and I'm ticked off too. He is such an asshole, so naturally here goes another argument. It never fails with us! We need to separate very soon because this isn't normal. Thankfully, he walks into the kitchen, giving me time to bite my tongue and wake up a little.

Opening the door, he lets me know he will be back in a little bit. Honestly, I don't care. I'm praying he will stay out. It's Saturday, which means he easily can find something, or someone, to do. I need to jump in the shower and then text Nolan to figure out what the game plan is for later. Let's see how Ty likes it when I don't come home or tell him where I'm at all night. You know what, I *want* him to come back home, just so he can get upset that I'm out and he doesn't have a single clue as to who I am with, or anything.

Seeing as it's only eleven o'clock in the morning, hearing my phone ring means it's anybody but Nolan. He never calls, he only texts me. I pick my phone up and read my mom's name. I answer the call in a chipper tone known as my "disguise voice."

"Hey, what's up?"

"What are you up to today, Aliza? Your father said he is going to be making a bunch of food tonight. If you want any, I'll tell him to put a plate aside, and you can bring it home or eat here," she says.

"Thanks, I definitely want some. I'm not sure if I am going to eat it there or take it home – for once I actually have plans," I say with excitement.

"What are you doing tonight? You and Tyler going out?"

"No, some people that Nolan and I know are getting together. I saw them at the store and they told us to stop by. Tyler's going to stay home tonight and do some stuff around the apartment." I feel bad lying, but it is what it is. If they knew the truth, their hearts would be broken. Most importantly, I worry that my Dad would go after Tyler and that he wouldn't be able to control himself…

"Well that sounds fun, just be careful. Text your dad later and let him know what your plans are. I'll talk to you later, I have to get to work."

I hate lying to my parents, but no need to make my life more hectic by letting them know that they were right this whole time. Making things more complicated than needed is another full-time job, one that I excel at. I need to get in the bathtub – being next to that asshole for even five minutes last night could have contaminated me. I'd rather be safe than sorry.

Do other people hate looking at themselves in the mirror, or is it just me? Every time I see my reflection, I pick out what I think is wrong with my face. Coincidently, I have decided that my whole face is wrong and I wish I could change it completely. At nineteen years old, I still have some freckles bridging my nose and scattered across my cheeks, and unfortunately the summer sun brings so many more out. Luckily, I love my hair. It is super long, almost to the bottom of my back, and I am always getting compliments on the length and color. The color isn't anything special, an awkward dark brown-but-nearly-black shade with no official name. Critiquing myself is the worst, I shouldn't do it, but I have an image problem. I can thank Tyler for most of this issue. His go-to comments when we are fighting consist of complaints about my thin figure. He is always telling me that I won't find someone to be with me for the reasons that he lists.

Wrapped in a towel, with half my face done up and the other half untouched, I hear someone walk through my front door.

"OH NO! My clothes are in the bedroom," I whisper to myself, considering I have no idea who is here.

"HELLLOOO?" I yelled through the closed bathroom door.

"It's just me," Nolan says.

What the hell… now I have to walk through my living room in order to get dressed. Right after, I just picked my image apart and stomped my self-esteem into the ground. The last person I want to see while I'm wrapped in a towel with half my face done is him. Inhale and run…

Standing in the kitchen doorway, he watches me book it towards my bedroom.

"Seriously? What was that all about?" he asks, laughing.

"Shut up. I left my clothes in the bedroom and it's cold in here." Kudos to me for the perfect cover-up.

"Are you ready to hear our options for tonight, girl?"

"Yes, I most certainly am…"

"There isn't shit going on tonight. The weather is too cold. That means we can hang out and drink here or go chill at one of my friend's houses. It's up to you. I don't give a shit what we do. I also scored some bottles, so we're set regardless."

"Awesome! I am almost done getting ready, so let's go chill at your house. I'm sick of being stuck here, and Ty said he is coming back after he gets some bud. He has no idea that I made plans. Actually, screw it – get me a big purse from my closet, so I can get ready at your place," I say in one breath.

"Do I look like your bitch?" he playfully asks.

"You *really* want me answer that?"

Even though he just flipped me off, he heads toward my closet. I hurry up and grab whatever I can fit into my arms. I need to hurry up and leave before Tyler gets back. I have a feeling that he will be here any minute. Once Nolan comes into the living room, I start tossing my make-up, curling iron, straightener, assorted hair and hygiene products, two pairs of shoes, some socks, my charger, yoga pants and a t-shirt all into the bag. I have no idea what we are doing tonight, so I need options.

Looking at me like I'm psychotic, Nolan says, "I don't remember telling you that you can move in. Why do you need all of this shit?"

"Listen, mind your own business. I'm ready, so let's head out," I say as nonchalantly as I can, grabbing my purse from the kitchen.

There is no reason my wallet should be open. Did I forget to close it last night after I threw the cigarette money in there from Nolan? I don't have time for this. I'll check it when I get over there. The winter weather is unbearable tonight. I don't mind being stuck at one of our places, as it currently doesn't sound like a bad idea. Our walk was quiet. Most of the time we kept the same pace and just stared straight ahead. I wonder if he thinks similar things as I do when it comes to us. It's like he never leaves my mind. I sound like an obsessed freak – I promise I'm not, though. Nolan and I would have such an awesome thing together, particularly since we click so effortlessly.

His voice startles me. "Watch your step, it's really slippery by my porch steps," he warns.

"Thanks for the warning. Knowing me I would have just busted my ass."

Following behind him, I can't help but smile for whatever reason – I'm not too sure. I watch him walk to the table off of the kitchen and notice that he has cut his hair.

He's all cleaned up and looks really good. He's the perfect height, has a nice body that goes perfectly with his face and his unique brown eyes that turn green sometimes, too. We like the same things, we're always laughing and we have fun together. I love that he can be completely laid-back one minute, then hyper and all over the place. Not to mention, the fact that he can make me laugh all day is enough for me.

Turning around, I look over and he's left the kitchen. I hear him in the bedroom off of the living room, putting some music on.

"Hey, if you want we can just chill here. I can make some drinks. It's so damn cold out and I'm not too sure how I feel about walking in that, bud," I said.

"Sounds good to me. You kind of overdressed, don't you think?" he says, teasing me.

"Probably not. You and I both know how our plans tend to change as quickly as they're made. With that being said, I do have to finish getting ready."

Without saying another word I walk upstairs and turn the bathroom light on. I'm actually in such an awesome mood. After about thirty minutes, I've finished my make-up, straightened my hair, put deodorant on and checked the finished product out in the mirror. Although I feel great, I'm still skeptical when it comes to how I look. Unfortunately, I'll never feel good enough for Nolan, mainly when I start to think about what his exes look like. Come on, there has to be a switch to turn this negativity off in my brain!

Personally, I don't think I got too dressed up. It's January after all, so you aren't catching me in any tiny dresses or skirts. I brought my favorite jeans because they really emphasize my curves and are a stone-washed material, so they look great with dark colors. I'm also wearing a black shirt and a cute open cardigan to go over my short-sleeved shirt. I love this sweater, it's crafted in a black-and-white Aztec pattern. Oh, and I can't forget my Bailey Bow UGGs, my go-to boots in winter. I never got into dressing like a hooker. I mean, I love my skirts and dresses in the summer, but definitely not when it's below thirty degrees! Who knows – maybe that's the reason he isn't into me?

"Yo, you almost done up there? It's not like we're going anywhere," he yells up the steps.

"Relax, killer. I'm just putting all my shit back into the bag."

Wait… that reminds me, I have to check my regular purse and make sure nothing is missing. I forgot that I noticed my wallet was wide open. Once I get downstairs, I throw my bag on the side of the couch, pick up my purse and immediately notice money missing.

"What a scumbag, man!" I yelled.

"What happened?"

"Tyler stole my money right out of my purse sometime this morning," I say, my voice shaking with anger.

"Did he take a lot?"

As I shut my purse, I let him know that Tyler took a little bit under half of what I had in there. Luckily, my checks are direct deposited into my account, so I take money out as needed. All I took out was eighty dollars; he left me with fifty dollars. Regardless, it isn't fair. I work for my money, despite the lousy job, and I don't bust my ass every day for him to steal it.

Nolan lights a cigarette for me and simply shakes his head. "He really still does have a stealing problem," he states.

"A big problem. Besides his shitty attitude, he's always buying weed and pills – on my account, apparently. He has no job and scrounges off of me and everyone else. I can't do this anymore."

"Forget it, screw 'em. I got you tonight, so don't worry about how much money you have left," he said.

"Thank you, and I appreciate it. I am just way over this shit."

"Grab two cups and follow me," he says as he walks into the other room.

Those few kind gestures from him make my heart skip and to anybody else, it wouldn't even be noticed when you have this close of a friendship, but for me, it always gives me a little hope. I don't know about Nolan, but I am getting *trashed* tonight. It has been a long time since I have been able to let loose. While I'm walking into the other room, I grabbed his aux off the kitchen table. I want the music blaring.

"Hook that speaker up to your phone and put on that good playlist," I told him.

"OK, boss."

CHAPTER 4

Three drinks in and I'm buzzed – like a nice kind of buzzed, though. Days in the East by Drake is playing on the aux and we're laughing, slamming our drinks and just chilling.

"Your phone's going off," Nolan says, as he hands me the phone.

Within a second my stomach drops: it must be Tyler. I know I said that I'll pull a "him" tonight, but I also have morals and tit-for-tat never solves anything.

Relieved once I look at it, I start to laugh. "Oh thank God, it's only my dad texting me."

"Fried food is done, Mom said you wanted a plate. Are you coming for it, or are you out?"

"Thanks, I'm still out. IDK what time I will be home, so I will grab it tomorrow. Thank you!!"

"Have fun. Be careful. Love you"

"love you too"

Text sent, I sound sober…nice. I put the phone back on the arm of the couch. I get up to grab Nolan's lighter and luckily that buzzed feeling is still there.

"Give me your lighter and let's do a shot," I demand.

"Oh OK, I forgot I have the master at handling liquor here," he says, reaching for the shot glasses.

"More like the master at everything."

Two shots are poured. He hands me my glass, takes his and we cheers at nothing in particular, too busy laughing. The liquor doesn't go down as badly as I thought it would. The more I drink, the smoother the shots go and the better the alcohol tastes.

"I have to go pee, I'll be right back," I tell him. I'm not stumbling yet, that's a plus. I sit down to pee, not even caring that the bathroom door is wide open, pull my pants up, then look in the mirror. Why do I let this stupid piece of glass control how I feel about myself? I'm not the most unattractive person – believe me, it could be worse. Ty's insults and the mirrors convince me that I am the worst-looking person there is, though. It makes no sense that I let an inanimate object and a selfish prick influence me to the point that I hate looking at myself. I am supposed to be enjoying myself, not stuck in this mirror pulling my soul intro shreds, yet again. As soon as I get back downstairs, I hear another voice come from the back room. Not gonna lie, I am kind of annoyed. Nolan never told me anyone was coming over.

"Hey, what's up?" I ask, walking into the room.

It's nobody special, just Shawn. He won't stay long, he never does. He mainly shows up out of the blue to smoke with everyone, then he goes home and does God knows what.

"Hey, how you been?" he replies.

"Oh you know, I been better, but nothing out of the ordinary. You hanging out for a little bit?"

As he hands the blunt to Nolan, Shawn shakes his head and shrugs his shoulders.

"Nah, I'm good, I'm going back home to chill. You guys enjoy whatever this is that is going on," he says sarcastically.

"Shut up, dude," Nolan snaps back.

I need another drink. I told myself I was actually going to drink tonight, so I'd better just sit back and enjoy this.

"You want a hit of this?" they ask, almost in unison.

"No…"

Half of my fourth drink is down and now I'm listening to these two talk about I-don't-even-know-what because following their conversations isn't easy. It isn't me, though, it's them. Currently lost in my phone, I do hear Shawn say "peace out". I look up and the door is shut, thank G   od!

"So, you done with your high time debates?" I ask Nolan.

"It's not a debate when you're right, and I was right," he claims.

We both hear my phone vibrate and look over. No shit, it's Tyler. My stomach curls into knots and I have no idea why. No matter what, I am not answering him. Wait – I'm not going to be completely immature, I'm just going to be extremely vague.

"Your boo is ringing you."

"I noticed. He can text me all he wants, but he doesn't need to know where I am. If he asks, I'm going to pull his card, the 'you're a psycho' because you want to know where I am and who I'm with. Doesn't that just sound ridiculous to even say, as someone's significant other?" I laugh out loud.

"Where are you?"

"helllllo"

"WTF I see that you read these texts, why aren't you answering me?"

I look up at Nolan, laugh and pull the famous Tyler card, kind of.

"Hey, I'm actually out with friends. Why, what's wrong?"

I don't realize Nolan is standing over me, but he has his eyes glued to the screen just like mine. It's like we are about to read some groundbreaking news through these texts. Of course, we are both just under the influence and finding entertainment in this.

"With WHO? You don't have any fucking friends besides Nolan. You've gone out with Nolan. Doing what?"

"Don't worry about who I'm with or where I am."

…just like that I power my phone down and throw it on the table. If my mom or anyone needs to get ahold of me, they have Nolan's number. They would call him before Tyler, anyway.

"You ready for the fight tomorrow, when you go home?" Nolan asks warily.

"Not really, but I'll figure it out tomorrow. Go get us another drink – I might as well make my last night alive count," I say, laughing.

"Might as well."

Within twenty minutes and two more drinks down, I trip over the chair, fell and decide I want to be the DJ. Oddly enough though, I kind of want to try and stay here, but then again that isn't the normal thing between us, so I know I have to sober up. If I asked, I know he wouldn't tell me no, but that's the thing, I'm afraid to ask. You would think that I would be comfortable to do, say or ask anything, considering how close we are, but I'm not. Having a thing for your best friend really makes life hard. Out of nowhere,

Nolan gestures for me to come into the kitchen, and by surprise I actually see food.

"I can cook when I want to, ya know. I made it before you came over. It's good," he says, handing me a piece of pizza.

"Yeah, right. Are you sure this wasn't frozen?"

I can't knock him; he can cook. When we were in high school he came to my house a little earlier than usual, and to my surprise, we went to his house and he immediately started making me eggs and toast.

I quickly swallow what I was chewing, wipe my mouth off and just sit there appreciating these little, weird things that he has always done for me.

I look over at him. "Do you remember when you made me breakfast that one morning before school?"

"Actually, yeah I do. Why?"

"I don't know if I ever told you or not, but I hate eating breakfast that early. I usually wait a few hours after I wake up to eat," I laugh.

"That's nice to know now, asshole," as he takes my lighter out of my hand.

"HEY, I ate half of that breakfast you made without a single complaint, so shut up!"

"You should feel lucky that I made you breakfast that early in the morning. No need to brag, but I'm like a master chef."

"Oh, are you? Well then the next time you come to my house, you can make dinner, Master Chef," I tell him with my famous eyeroll.

"I'm sure Tyler would love to walk in and see me cooking dinner for you. He already gets pissy when he comes home and sees me there doing nothing."

"When he does come home… not like that's often anymore. He's just ridiculous. I will never understand why he gets pissed off."

He exhales and says, "You're always real giddy and stuff when I'm around. I notice it, and I'm sure he does, too."

I wasn't expecting that. In all honesty, I almost fall out of my chair. At this point, I don't even know what to say. If he notices how I get, then why doesn't he address it? There is no way he can't tell that I'm head over heels for him. Can I go crawl into a corner and die now?

"Ew, no I don't… it's just cool to have someone around after being by myself or aggravated by him. You could send anybody over and I'd get overly excited… life as a hermit, bud." I hope that was convincing.

"Whatever you say," he says sarcastically.

I have to change this subject fast. I really need to move on because neither of these men are going to work out. I know Tyler isn't going to be a thing much longer in my life, but I always had this little bit of hope for Nolan and I. The thing is, the friendship that we created isn't worth losing, ultimately due to a bad break-up. I've seen people date and ruin their friendship; it happened a dozen times alone within my circle of friends.

"Regardless what he thinks, I pay all the bills there. I'm the only one who cleans or buys things for the apartment. Therefore, *I* make the rules, not Tyler, so if I want you to make dinner, than guess who's making dinner... you," I say in a serious tone.

"Listen, I get it. And if you want dinner, I'll make you dinner every day this week. Throw in breakfast, too... wait, not breakfast. I'll do lunch, because your bitch ass doesn't eat breakfast."

"I'll believe that when it happens. In the meantime, I'm going to enjoy this frozen pizza and these drinks before I have to head home."

"Stop playing with that frozen pizza shit. I really did make this," he says, hurt.

My phone has been turned off for hours. I should probably turn it back on. Dreading the amount of ignorant texts that will be streaming in, I turn it on anyway. Not only did he send me an additional six texts, he even left a *voicemail*. A voicemail that I'm deleting before I listen to it because I know whatever he felt the need to say, isn't going to be nice.

"How many texts did you get from crazy?" Nolan asks.

"Six texts, plus a voicemail that I already deleted without listening to. I already know that whatever he said isn't going to be kind, so it isn't worth listening to when I know I'm going to get upset."

Nolan looked at me for a minute, then says, "I don't know why he acts like this. You do a lot for him, and he takes it for granted."

I can't say I heard Nolan talk in a sympathetic way regarding my relationship in a while. I don't know whether to believe he cares, but it seems like he obviously pays attention more then he lets on. Our past is hectic and it puts us in weird spots with one another here and there, which means we don't always say and do what we want to. It's kind of like the fear of crossing boundaries that neither of us really have for each other. The boundaries that I don't like to cross on his end, I made up – and I feel like he did the same for me.

I sighed. "We live and we learn... like I learned to avoid certain things that will set him off. Regardless, he and I won't be lasting too much longer. I let it be known."

"What's your plan if you leave him?"

"I don't know, stay single? Who knows. I don't think I can do this relationship thing. Maybe I'll find a friend with benefits or someone I can call when I need something. Then just send them home afterwards," I say to see his reaction.

With an awkward smirk he replies, "Word."

What kind of smirk was that? I'm not really sure if I even received that look before. Was it a good look or a bad look? This whole thing is killing me! All I want to do is grab him and tell him he's a damn moron for not being able to see that I want to be with him, but I'll keep playing the role of the not-interested asshole, like I have been for years… yes, *years*.

CHAPTER 5

"Oh my God, why is it so cold out? I thought drunk people don't feel the cold?" I ask Nolan.

"Why wouldn't a drunk person feel the cold?! Where the hell did you come up with that? Drunk, high, awake, asleep… a person is going to feel the cold or heat," he says, laughing at me.

"Okay know-it-all, my bad."

"Pay attention before you bust your ass, it's all icy. You're lucky I'm not an asshole, because I could have let you walk home by yourself. You wouldn't even be able to make it there."

Sarcastically speaking and still drunk, I say, "Why thank you, sir, for your fine services tonight."

"You don't have the slightest idea about all the services I provide," he says, with that smirk again.

"What's up with that expression? That's the second time I seen you make that weird-ass smirk!"

Acting stupid, he says he doesn't know what I'm talking about. But there's a reason for that smirk and the ridiculous part is, I don't want to set myself up for false hopes here, but I swear he is up to something. Some kind of no-good motive that I actually am kind of liking, now that I keep thinking about it. Although people say history shouldn't be repeated, I am definitely up to the challenge, in order to dispute that claim.

"Thanks for walking me home, but I'm good here. I should be able to make it," I say while stumbling.

"I'm at least walking you to your porch," he says.

"This is why you're my best friend – you're awesome!"

"I can't disagree there," he jokes.

"I'll text you tomorrow or something, I'm going in and jumping right into bed," I mumble.

"Alright, I'll see ya tomorrow."

I lock the door behind me, turn the light on and kick my shoes off at the door. Shit, I forgot my bag at Nolan's.

Once I put my purse down, I notice Tyler sitting on the couch, all pissed off. He looks at me, lights up a cigarette and starts up with me instantly.

"Did you and your *buddy* have fun together?"

"Seriously, I'm not doing this tonight."

"Obviously, you're not doing much with me, because you're too busy kissing Nolan's ass," he spits.

"First of all, stop with the past shit. It's the only thing you can hold over my head. Why do you have to bring pointless shit up?" At this moment, I'm beyond pissed.

"If you think I only have one thing I can hold over your head, you really are an idiot."

I lost it. "Excuse me? You don't get to take things from my past and twist them into a story that makes me look bad. Do NOT threaten me with the choices I made. There isn't anything that you can tell people that they don't already know. Considering the source, they won't buy into your bullshit anyway, so nice try. Have fun with all of that," I snap, while glaring into his eyes.

Before I can shut my mouth, I feel a sudden tightness around my neck and a lack of oxygen to my lungs. I try to let a wail out, but not a sound is made. In a blind panic, I begin to kick my legs around and swing my fists at him.

He starts to squeeze harder, "You better think again, bitch! If you don't think I can ruin your cute little friendship with him, or anybody else for that matter, you are on good drugs. You can kiss your little buddy goodbye, simply by you putting your little front on over the years. I will sabotage your fake friendship!" he screams into my face.

With a swift move of his wrist, he throws me into the wall. My blood is boiling, and I know if I open my mouth again, he will hurt me way more than he just did.

"Keep thinking you can do whatever you want with him," he grinned.

"Do what you want, Tyler. I don't fucking care."

Classic. I slam the door, get undressed and crawl under my blankets, crying. All I want to do is run into the living room and punch him in his face so hard. Obviously I won't, but I want to more than anything. But the consequences of that isn't worth the few seconds of enjoyment that I will get. Plus, I just heard the front door slam. He can go out and not disclose any information to me at all, it's totally okay… such double standards. Sleep isn't going to happen on my watch anytime soon. Awkwardly, I gravitate towards my journal. It is weird how writing makes me feel more at ease. I wasn't expecting this to catch on this fast. I guess it's better than picking up my phone and starting more shit.

Entry #74

My great night has turned into ~~bullshit~~ MEGA BULLSHIT! I should have just summoned up the courage to ask Nolan if I could crash there. He would never say no. This is so stupid that I am afraid to say or ask things like that. I am so worried about making it seem like I have a thing for him, although he can already tell. That's another thing that kind of upset me, too!!! He knows I have some sort of feelings for him but chooses to ignore them. WHY?! Obviously that answer is easy... he isn't into me the way that I am into him. Knowing that makes me so annoyed. Am I being played by him, too?

As much as I don't want to get into details right now, it's probably best I fill you in. If for any reason someone comes across this journal and reads it, they may think I'm insane, since I am acting like an inanimate object is a person. Anywho, Nolan and I were super close and we did EVERYTHING together. We were with each other all day, every day. It was like that for years. There isn't another person in the world who clicks with me as well as he does – believe me, there isn't a single soul who could match the bond we have. I have never met anybody who can make me laugh or who I even enjoy doing nothing with. We just have fun all of the time. People always thought we dated because we just had this glow to us when we were together. I actually didn't even want to meet him because I hate meeting new people, but I was tricked into it by mutual friends.

One day before the end of our summer vacation, we decided that we were going to have a blast before school started. Out of all the friends in our circle at that point in time, we never needed to have many people with us; "we" were our circle, and Shawn tagged along. So Nolan, Shawn and I played it off like we were going to the movies, so I could stay out later. I had the earliest curfew. My mom had just bought me school sneakers and school clothes, with both pairs of shoes being Jordans. I was so excited to be able to stay out a little later and since we were getting drunk, I was even happier. I know that at 15 years old, it's probably not something I should have loved so much, but it was my favorite thing to do. I took a shower, crimped my hair, and threw on a white shirt, the tightest pink Dickies I owned and my pink-and-white sneakers.

Nolan and Shawn came to my house, sat outside with my mom, and told her that Shawn's brother was going to the arcade with his gf, so he was our ride there and back. After convincing her, we started to walk to Shawn's house. There were no rules there: we could drink and do anything we wanted. My folks would never let us do anything like that.

It was a normal fun- and alcohol-filled night. I mean, me being in that condition wasn't anything out of the ordinary, considering I was a teenage alcoholic. However, all I remember was looking towards Shawn, sitting on his bed, and then that was the end of that. Nolan actually started to kiss me. As drunk as I was, I was in heaven, literally.

I took every bit of him in with every sense that I had. It was complete lust. To be honest with you, nothing can compare to the euphoria that I had while Nolan took complete control of me. I don't know if you really want to hear all the graphic details, but I'm sure you can conclude that we had sex. He wasn't the first guy that I messed with like that.

I'm not one of those girls who wants rose petals thrown on the floor or anything. Don't get me wrong, there are a few details that I'd like to change about that night, but I won't get too far with that at this point. Unfiltered, messy, illegal, full of lies, and alcohol... that was my life. Nolan and I try not to mention what happened that night. That was the messiest, wonderful time of my life with all of my friends. We all had crazy memories that year.

Truly,

All is fair in lust & war

Oh my God, my head hurts so badly. I need Tylenol *and* a drink. What the hell time is it, and where is my phone? AGH! I really don't want to get out of bed to find that stupid thing, but I have to. Cracking my bedroom door open, I see Tyler sleeping on the couch. Better him than me. What he started last night was uncalled for, and I still haven't told Nolan about the drama. It sounds weird, but there are some things I don't want to tell him because I don't want him to think he is the reason for my relationship issues with Tyler. I fear that Nolan will take a few steps back to give us "room for improvement". Our relationship problems are way more than just having Nolan around. Tyler is the one who created these trust issues with his lies, disappearing and constant disrespect. Wait! I forgot about him stealing my goddamn money yesterday, too!

CHAPTER 6

Walking into the kitchen to get a drink and two Tylenol, I see Tyler's phone on the kitchen countertop. Trust is a shifty thing between two people and invading privacy solves nothing, but when you are the one always getting hurt, you have your reasons.

I grab his phone, unlock it and start with his call log. Nothing out of the ordinary... Aliza, Mom, Aliza, Aliza, Mom, Jason, Mom, etc. On to the next step: his text messages. With a deep breath and a peek around the walkway, I open his texts up. Then I see it: "Maria".

"Who the hell is Maria?" I say to myself.

Before I even open the texts between him and this Maria, I can feel my face burning up and a whole lot of anxiety building up in my chest. At this point I want to take this phone and smash it on the floor, but I have to see what's in these messages.

Clicking it open, I scroll through and there the truth is in black and white that he's cheating on me. These messages between them are filled with sexting, dirty pictures, and time and dates to meet up. I can't decide if the flirty texts or the dirty pictures are worse, but what I do know is that I need to figure out how to handle all of this! Quickly, I grab my phone from my hoodie pocket and start taking pictures of his phone with these messages displayed so that I have proof. To think he actually got mad because I left my house for a few hours to have drinks for the first time in months, he is out of his mind! When approaching this issue I'm going to need a plan, so I need to just sit on this for a little bit before I say anything.

Even though I have said it and thought it a million times, seeing the actual proof doesn't make me anymore angrier. In retrospect I always knew this would happen. Also, I kind of prayed it would happen hoping he would just leave me for some girl. He's lucky that he is still asleep only because I'm annoyed more than angry… I think. I walk into my bedroom and send a quick text to my friend Ally. She's been my friend for a few years, probably the only friend besides Nolan that I kept in contact with since being with Ty. Not even forty seconds go by and she tells me she will be picking me up and to fill her in on the drama. I have to jump in the shower fast and get dressed; sweats, UGGs and a hoodie sound good to me. My drive to look like an upstanding citizen is non-existent.

My hair's full of shampoo, my phone won't stop going off and I just dropped the damn conditioner bottle. I rinse all that crap out my hair, rip the shower curtain open, throw a towel on and check my phone.

"Yo I'm out front. You ready?" Ally texted me after calling me seven times.

"Throwing clothes on, be out in 2 minutes" SEND…

Look who finally woke up. I don't even want to look at his sorry ass. Right into the bedroom I go, throw my wet hair in a bun, get dressed and stroll out the door. I probably shouldn't start, but it's my turn to be in the right.

"Boy, we have A LOT to talk about when I decide to come back," I say in a condescending tone.

"Okay like what?" Wow, he really has no idea.

And just like that, I slam the door and I run into Ally's car.

Ally turned the music down. "What is going on with you and Tyler?" she asks.

"Still no job, still a thief – which shit, I forgot to mention that I know he stole my money. Plus, I went out to Nolan's for a couple hours, had a couple of drinks, still came home and he instantly started his shit with me because I turned my phone off. If I ask where he is, then I'm a *psycho*, so who is he to ask me anything? Most importantly, the dumbass left his phone on the counter and I went through it. I found dirty texts and pictures from some Maria. Wait until you stop the car and look at these!"

Damn, I said all that in one breath. I need a cigarette. Thank God Ally has a lighter in her car, because naturally I forgot mine.

"Well, I hope you aren't like surprised that he is talking to somebody. You and I both know he was up to no good, and unfortunately you had to find out like this. What did Nolan say about any of this?"

"I didn't even talk to him yet. He's still sleeping – we got trashed last night," I tell her.

"Forward all the pictures of Tyler's phone to my phone so I can check all them out. He is such an asshole. I don't know why he thinks he can pull something over on you. You always find out. Like the time he tried to be slick and get with me when you guys were broken up – like I wasn't going to tell you! He's beyond stupid."

Oh, that's right. I forgot about the time he tried to get with one of my best friends – who does that? The funny part is Ally only dealt with him because she respects me;

other than that she doesn't like him either. I love Ally to death, but she can be a bitch, which is why we were both in shock that he attempted that. She was never really nice to him. Ally's pretty. She is kind of tall, with dark hair and a nice body, compared to mine. I look like a teenager, but she looks like a grown-ass woman. I get a little jealous since her boobs are way bigger, but I learned to live with what I don't have. She looks like she can be 25. She has always looked older than everyone else, but in a good way.

"Can we stop at a Burger King or something? I'm starving?" I beg.

"That does sound good right now."

"Thank you. We can just go to the drive-thru, I don't even care."

After I give my order and get Nolan a meal, I notice my phone vibrating from a text. Tyler.

"Stop playing your games and tell me WTF is going on?"

A couple of things could be done to approach this. I can:

1. Tell him via text
2. Ignore him
3. Send him my photos of his phone that I took.

"Ally, should I entertain this or just wait until I go home? I can do this one of three ways, via text, send the pics or ignore him."

With a quick answer, "You should maybe do it over text, 'cause you know he is going to explode. Then again, doing it that way can make it even worse with him. He is so unpredictable… like I don't even know how you should go about this. Whatever you choose, be careful, and I'm serious. I'll even come with you if you want to do it face-to-face. It'd be safer," she says with a look of concern.

"I'll figure it out after you drop me off at Nolan's, so I can get my bag and give him this food before it gets gross."

Life is a joke. Karma is supposed to keep people in check and I feel like the more I try to do well, the more bad karma I get. Nothing makes much sense anymore. Do the good guys really finish last?

Ally pulls up to Nolan's. "Make sure you text me later, so I know what happens with Tyler." She gives me a tight hug.

"Don't worry. I doubt he'll put up a fight. Clearly he has other things in his life that he's more concerned about," I tell her before I shut her car door.

"Shit, I should have texted Nolan," I say when I noticed the door's locked, so I attempt to call him.

Surprisingly, he answers on the fourth ring, sounding sleepy.

"Open your door, I'm here. I left my bag here last night, and I have BK for you."

Before I even hang up, he opens the door. I hand him the bag of food and sit down.

"What's up with you?" he asks.

"Where should I start? When I got home last night, Tyler started his shit, flipped my living room table – it's broken now. Then this morning, I saw his phone on the counter and I went through it. He's been cheating on me. Look at this shit," I say while tossing my phone over to him.

Tossing my phone back, Nolan says, "He's not worth the shit you're going through. Unless you get rid of this shit now, welcome to the rest of your life. You know as well as I know, he will never stop. He will never change."

Nolan and his statement threw me off. Speechless, I didn't know what to say. Does he actually give a shit?

"Easier said than done," I state.

"Easier to go through this every single day? Easier to find bitches on his phone and whatever else he does to you behind your back? Use your head. You're not stupid."

"My bad. I don't know how to be alone. I have been with him for how long now? It isn't that easy," I say, pissed off.

"I'm not saying this to get you mad, but there's no reason to keep putting yourself through this with someone that isn't worth it. He doesn't deserve you. And you don't deserve this."

He's right. He cares. He isn't being an asshole. He is just trying to help. He still has no idea that I want to kick my shoes off, turn my phone off and stay here with him all day.

"Do you care if I chill here for a bit? He knows Ally picked me up a bit ago. I'm just going to act like I'm with her still, so I can send these pictures. Like she said, if I do it in person, he is going to explode."

He hands me what's left of his cigarette, "I don't know why you even ask me, and yes you can stay here."

"Well, I don't know… I don't want to get in the way or make you feel awkward about brining certain people over.

"Who would be coming over that would make me not want you to stay here?" he asked.

"I don't know, I'm just saying... relax."

"Regardless of who I have come here or who I hang out with, they're not going to make me stop talking to you or hanging out with you. It never worked before, so it ain't ever going to work in the future."

"Thank you," I say.

I should probably say something else, but I can't at this moment. I'm taken back by the fact that he does care; at least it sounds like he does. This friendship is the worst and the best all at once.

With a deep breathe, I go into my inbox, click Ty's name and start selecting the pictures that I need to send to him. No, wait – I have a better idea. I cancelled the pending message and decide to confront him first.

"Not only did I see you steal money out of my purse last night, I found out about more shit."

Now, to wait for his lies because he won't admit anything. For some reason, I can't take my eyes off the message box. I see the three dots in the corner, which means he is texting me. As each second passes by, I am getting even more pissed off. With a quick vibrate, his text comes through.

"IDK what you're talking about. I didn't steal any money. Maybe your buddy did it, since he was the only one over here that I know of. Oh yeah, what else did you find out? Plz fill me in, I'd love to know!!"

Not realizing Nolan is standing over my shoulder reading these texts, he clears his throat and startles me. "I would never in my life take your goddamn money. He needs to chill with that shit!"

"Nolan, I know that. I trust you more than anybody. This is his blame game, and you're always the first one he drags into it. I think he tries to get me mad at you and that will never work," I inform him.

"Nolan would NEVER steal a dime from me, nice try! What did I find out? I found out why you haven't been coming home at night and why you have been such a dick, more so than usual. Next time you plan on cheating on me, make sure you can trust the girl first."

"OK psycho, here you go with your insecurities and made-up stories. Nobody's cheating on you, even though I SHOULD because you don't do a fucking thing for me. You don't even sleep in the same bed as I

do, let alone do anything else to me or for me."

"OH MY GOD! I cannot do this with him anymore. I know I shouldn't pull this card, but I am going to… he lies all the time. What's one little lie from me going to impose on this already screwed-up situation?!" I yell.

"Don't try to pull the insecurity card, asshole. Your little sidepiece came out and told me everything. So you can either A) Come clean and admit to your selfish ways or B) Keep your charade going and shit is really going to hit the fan."

I am at the point that I'm shaking. He lies so much and he's just going to lie his ass off some more. I should just send these pictures and get to the bottom of this shit.

"What should I do? Send the pictures and just tell him I contacted her after I saw these? I already lied and said this bitch told me everything." I look to Nolan for advice.

"I guess. You know, if you don't stick to your story he's going to show everyone and act like you're the crazy one who is making it all up."

"True."

Selecting all these pictures to send to him makes me realize how much time I have put into this relationship for nothing. I have been paying all the bills, financially taking care of a grown man while being walked all over, used and abused. I am DONE.

"Maria came clean, so it doesn't matter if you choose to lie. FYI, I seized the opportunity to go through your phone; you left it on the counter last night. You are caught, and I am DONE. We are DONE. There is no more 'me and you' – obviously there hasn't been for a while, since you just thought you would have your cake and eat it too. Guess what? Nobody gets to have their

cake and eat it too, except for ME. You have one week to get your shit out of MY apartment. If I were you, I'd probably find somewhere to sleep tonight, because I do NOT want you in MY home. You make me sick!"

I put the phone down, walk in the kitchen and let Nolan know that I will be staying the night. Other than running home to grab clothes and something to eat, I don't really want to be there. I know Tyler will purposely stay home tonight and that's fine, since I won't be there.

"I would wait a little bit before going to your crib. You know he is going to snap because you just left him," Nolan warns.

"I'll leave in an hour or so. He'll get over it, since he has no choice. If he cared, he would have never put himself and me in this position. I am too good to him. I don't deserve this." The tears start flowing.

"Truest thing I've heard you say. Don't cry. He's not something worth crying over. You had to know this day was coming."

"I'm just upset that I let this happen. These tears aren't because it's over, these tears are for the time I friggin' wasted on him and this half-assed relationship."

Out of nowhere, I feel arms wrap around me and I start crying even more. Here I am at nineteen years old crying to my close friend, over some asshole who played me like a fiddle. How is this even my life? Although this moment has me feeling pretty down, being embraced by Nolan is what I need. It's what I've always needed.

"Thank you for being here through every bit of shit that goes on in my life, Nolan. I appreciate it more than you know. I'm serious," I say to him.

Looking down at me, we lock eyes for a minute and he hugs me tighter. Before letting go he says, "You don't have to thank me. You do enough for me."

CHAPTER 7

Rather than add more fuel to the fire, I figured I'd wait a little bit before going home. I accidentally fell asleep and instead of waking me up, Nolan just let me sleep for almost four hours straight. I needed that nap, but I wish I didn't take it. I hate walking in the dark because it's freezing out! I have to put layers on so I don't freeze – the only problem is I don't have layers since I left in a rush with Ally earlier. All I threw on was my coat and hat.

"Hey, give me one of your hoodies – it's freezing out."

"Go upstairs and grab one of my North Face hoodies out of the closet. They're the warmest," Nolan says.

While I ran up the steps, I thanked him, grabbed a hoodie from the closet, threw it on and grabbed my bag. I contemplate leaving the bag full of stuff here, but I kind of need it so I can fill it with clothes. My other bags and backpacks are too small.

"Make sure your phone's charged. I feel like it probably isn't a good idea to go over there. You should just wait until tomorrow," Nolan says.

"I can't. I left my wallet there and everything. The last thing I need is for him to grab my bank card and God knows what else I have laying around. I mean, I hid the wallet, so let's hope he hasn't found it."

"Try not to argue with him. You know shit is going to hit the fan. Here, take a key, so you have it to get in when you get back. Lock the door behind you, too. I'm going upstairs to chill until you get back. Hopefully nothing happens, but if it does, you need to call me," he says.

Finally bundled up, I grab the key and lock the door behind me. It's bitterly blustery out and as much as I'm dreading this walk, it can't last long enough. I'm not looking forward to running into Ty because it's not going to turn out well. It only takes fifteen minutes to get from Nolan's to my house. Tonight, it feels like I'll be there in five minutes. Eerily, it is so silent and there doesn't seem to be a soul out. It is putting me more on edge than I already am. The sky is cloudy, I can barely see a single star, but the moon is full, bright and in full sight.

I seriously don't want to do this. I walk up to the house and see the windows full of light on the side of the house, which means he must be home. Any other night he is gone, but tonight he stays home. I hate him! I walk in, and there he is…

"Took you long enough to get home," he says.

"I didn't know I was on a time limit, considering we are no longer together. I didn't come to my home to argue with you. I came to grab some things and go, since you won't leave, evidently."

He slowly gets off the couch and walks over by the front door, locking it and standing right in front of it with his psychotic sneer. "You aren't going anywhere until we talk about this. There was no reason for you to go through my phone."

"Excuse me! You aren't going to tell me when and if I can leave. As a matter of fact, you aren't going to try and blame me for our relationship ending. You lied, you stole, you didn't do your part and it caught up to you, but it just so happens your phone was going off," I say to him in a calm manner.

"Go ahead, try and leave, Aliza… see what happens. Until this is talked out, you won't be going anywhere like I just said a minute ago. If I were you, I wouldn't worry about filling your bag. I would go sit down, so we can talk this out," he demands.

I have to try and sneak my phone out to text Nolan because this isn't going to end well. If Tyler sees my phone, he might smash it. I have to wait until he isn't looking. Scared isn't the word to use for my state right now. I am fucking terrified. To make matters worse, I smell liquor on his breath. I quickly throw some stuff into my bag; I don't have time to empty it. I grab my wallet and my journal and tuck those items underneath everything, so he doesn't seem them. He might just try to kill me tonight.

Walking past him to throw some food in the bag, he grabs my arm in the kitchen door way.

"Tyler, let me go NOW," I yell.

"I was nice about this two times already. If you aren't going to sit down and talk to me, I will fucking *make* you. The option is yours. You should have kept your hands off of my phone. Instead, you went though it because you're insecure… You caused this and you're going to figure it out, whether you like it or not," he screams into my face.

In one pull, he throws me onto the couch. I have to get out of here, but there's no way I'm going to be able to. He isn't going to take his eyes or his hands off of me, apparently.

"What can we possibly have to talk about, Tyler? You have been cheating on me. I let it go, so you can do the same," I beg.

"We have a lot to talk about, like how you lied to me last night and got drunk and probably screwed Nolan behind my back. Then you go through my phone today and leave all day without telling me where the fuck you have been? It doesn't work like that!"

I have nothing to say to you! LEAVE ME ALONE," I yell, while clawing to get off the couch.

Then it happened. With an instant sting and something wet dripping down my chin, I feel blood and realized he open-hand smacked me on the lip.

"Sit down and shut the hell up or you're just going to make this worse," he commands.

I don't know whether to speak, try to get up or hit him back. Regardless of what I choose to do, it's going to happen again. If I don't say a word, he's going to hit me. If I say something that he doesn't want to hear, he's going to hit me. Last, but not least, if I try to leave, he is going to hit me… or worse. I have to get to my phone and at least call Nolan or Ally and leave it the call running, so they can hear. So, there's proof. He isn't going to take his eyes off of me long enough to text or talk on the phone. I have to think of a plan.

"You busted my lip. Get away from me and let me go into the bathroom," I say as I shove him away from me.

"I'll sit right here until you're done, but you still aren't leaving until we talk about what you did," he still attempts to reason with me.

I have never met a narcissist like him in my life. He is extremely mental and needs help. There is no way he can make this my fault. However, he will find a way to turn this on me, story of my life – not for long, though. I'm not going to attempt to shut the bathroom door because that might trigger him to get up and walk in. With the water running and one hand purposely knocking things over so it doesn't seem like I'm on my phone, I text Nolan.

"Help now"

In the nick of time I am able to get the phone back in my pocket without him seeing. His reflection appears in the bathroom mirror, while he watches me hold a wet washcloth over my swollen, busted, and bleeding lip.

"Are you going to sit down and talk now?" he asks.

"Do I have a goddamn choice?!" I yell while I walk into the living room.

I feel my phone vibrating nonstop; thank God I have the ringer off. I hope he understands that I cannot answer it. He needs to get here immediately because this is going to get worse.

"Why did you go through my phone, knowing it would cause an argument? That's all you know how to do is get into people's business! Business that doesn't involve you. You love the drama!"

"I knew you were up to something because I caught you in so many damn lies! I'm not an idiot. You haven't been coming home, and that usually means one thing!"

He slams his hand on the table. "It doesn't mean shit. It means you don't pay attention to me at all. You don't spend time with me, you're too busy with your social life," he says.

"What social life?! I have two friends. Nobody else talks to me because of you! Would you want to be around me or be intimate with me if I fucking abused you in any way I could think of?! Leave me alone! Go be with Maria … whoever she is. I do not want to continue this relationship. Why can't you understand that?!"

Again, an instant pain ensues, except this time he sent the lighter flying across the room and it hit me in the shin. That hurt worse than the blow to the face. Do I deserve this? How can this happen to a person if they don't deserve this? What have I done wrong in my life to endure such an abusive relationship? I have to do something quick. Luckily, I'm still in my boots and didn't take my coat off yet. My bag is in the middle of the living room. I dropped it on my way to the kitchen, when I wanted to grab some food. I need to figure out how to distract him or do something so it catches him off guard long enough for me to grab it and escape to the front door.

"Am I allowed to go in the kitchen and grab something frozen to put on my lip, or are you going to hit me again?" I ask cautiously.

"I don't give a shit. I deserve an apology for the shit you pulled last night, and for you sneaking through my phone. If you stayed out of my messages, we wouldn't be fighting like this."

Does he hear himself speak? He deserves an apology for what I did to him? He has been cheating and physically harming me, and yet he somehow deserves an apology because I deal with this and then found out. Basically in his eyes, we wouldn't be arguing if I never caught him. In his deranged mind, we aren't arguing because he cheated on me, or the fact that he doesn't tell me where he is, who he is with or anything. The nights he doesn't spend at home, the abuse or his shitty attitude, none of that is the reason we are fighting either, apparently.

"You know what, I shouldn't have gone through your phone, you're right. I apologize for going through your phone, I'm sorry. Can we please stop fighting? I'm exhausted and didn't sleep well. I want to lay down," I say, attempting to calm him until I can leave.

"Do you actually mean your apology, or is it to shut me up?"

"Obviously I mean it, or I wouldn't even waste my breath. Are we done now?" I ask.

"Yes, we are. That was all I wanted. I'm happy you see that you were wrong. Hopefully you learn to trust me and stop acting on your insecurities."

I can't do this. I have to wait at least five minutes to be in the clear. As soon as he turns his back and walks into another room, I am booking it through that door and down those steps. He thinks I gave in and he won, so that will buy me some time to do this. In the meantime, I have to devise a plan to keep the peace and his suspicions low.

"Did you take my charger by any chance? It's not a big deal, it just isn't in the bedroom."

"No, I have mine right here." He holds his up to show me.

"Oh shit, I might have dropped it getting out of Ally's car, I think. It's so cold, I don't even want to go check."

"I'm not checking. Wait to use mine when I'm done, "he orders.

"It's fine, mine has been dead for a while now. If it isn't on the porch or the inside steps, screw it," I say.

Quietly, I grab my bag and slide it by the door. He went into the bathroom to piss, so I'd better seize the moment.

"I'm going to see if it's in front of the house," I yell from the front door.

Without another word spoken, I grab my bag, slam the door and book it down the steps. Halfway down the driveway, I hear him screaming from the bedroom window.

"If you think you're going to avoid this, Aliza, you're wrong! I'm not going anywhere, so the joke's on you, bitch," he yells out the window.

Once I get in the clear, I take my phone out and see ten texts from Nolan and four missed calls. I call him back and oddly enough, I see him down the street.

"Is that you down the road?" I ask.

"Obviously."

I laugh and hang up. At least he *tried* to rescue me. However, I am usually my own hero; 99.9% of the time, I'm too headstrong to ask for help. In return, my quick wits and strength have been trained over the years, although none of this is right. As a female, there is no reason that I should have to learn how to fight, so I can protect myself from someone who should be protecting me, rather than hurting me.

"We should probably just get to your house, because I have a feeling he is going to be leaving, especially trying to figure out where I went because he's going to try to catch me," I warn Nolan.

"How bad did it get?"

Bad. You'll see when we get in the light."

Focusing on my face, he says, "I don't need to be in the light – I can see your fat lip."

I feel my phone vibrate. I pull it out and see a text from my dad.

"Everything okay? Heard yelling from your apartment."

The joys of my parents living about five houses away. I never liked living this close to my parents, since I feel like I have to hide everything about my relationship for some reason. I'm not sure if it's embarrassment, feeling like I let them down or seeming like a liar. The fighting is getting too out of hand, and I don't think I can keep this under wraps much longer.

"I'm not even home! I wonder what is going on!"

"Who is that?" Nolan asks.

"It's my dad. He heard Tyler yelling and wanted to make sure everything is okay. I'm not sure if he knew it was Tyler or not. Whatever the case is, I told him that I'm not home, which is half of the truth. What they don't know won't hurt 'em," I say.

"Be careful if you are out. I'll keep an eye on the place while you're gone."

"Always. Thank you."

I slide my phone into my coat pocket and take my cigarettes and lighter out. It's so cold that I can't even feeling the smoke when I inhale, let alone exhale it. I feel bad for lying to my parents about my disastrous relationship with Tyler, but they're so dramatic. I always made him look so good even when they had their suspicions. Sadly, my pride is more important than my safety and I don't want to look like an idiot. I hate the "I told you so" situations. It doesn't take a rocket scientist to notice Tyler is an unmotivated, entitled, ignorant piece of shit.

"Let me get some of that cigarette, I forgot mine at the house. As soon as I saw your text, I threw on whatever was in front of me. I don't even know if I have a clean shirt on," he says, laughing.

"Yeah, I'm sorry. I should have just waited, but I didn't need him finding my journal or stealing my bank card. At least the worst is over. Now I just have to worry about how he is going to retaliate. I don't think I should stay at my apartment for a couple of days. If I do go there, I'm going to need someone sleeping over."

I hand him what is left of my cigarette. "Listen Aliza, you don't have to apologize to me, but you really shouldn't stay there by yourself for at least the next two or three days. His mind hasn't grasped that you left him yet. So when it does, you know he is going to go berserk. Tyler has some screws loose in his head as it is," Nolan says.

"I'll figure something out. Obviously I'm going to stay at your place tonight, and I'll see if I can crash at Ally's tomorrow night and the night after."

"Why ask Ally? You can crash at my place for as long as you need. I don't give a shit."

"I don't want to intrude on your life, bud. I mean, don't you think it'll be a little weird with me staying at your place in case you have plans with people?" I ask.

As we get to his door, he fixes me with an awkward glare, "if you're saying all this because you think you're going to get in the way of me and whatever girl I'm talking to, chill. I have nothing going on this week; I don't plan on any bitches coming over, and you being okay is all I'm focused on at this point, so stop talking. Let my mind have some time to relax, considering I have to put up with you staying here for a few days," he demands in a joking tone.

All I can do is shake my head. God, he can be such a dick! I know he is helping and that he cares, but he could have been a little more sensitive! On the other hand, my life falling apart because I have a psychotic ex-boyfriend really doesn't seem that bad. Being able to crash at Nolan's for two or three nights is something that I have no complaints about, except he has like no food. I'll take care of that tomorrow, though. Once we get in the house, I kick my shoes off, throw my coat in the corner and place my bag on the table.

"I'm about to jump in the shower. I have such a bad chill from that walk. Where do you want me to put my stuff?" I ask.

"It doesn't matter to me. Throw it in my bedroom, by the dresser."

CHAPTER 8

I did exactly what he told me to do – I threw my bag in Nolan's bedroom, next to the dresser. Locking the bathroom door behind me, I caught a glimpse of my lip in the mirror. Not only was there a split in my lip, it was also swollen and red. Abuse doesn't look good on anybody, but for unknown reasons, some women (such as myself) keep this look for years before they do something about it.

I will not be a statistic. My self-image is barely recognizable to myself when I look in the mirror anymore. Not only have I lost my bubbly personality, my happiness and drive in life, I have let myself go due to the depression and stress from all the shit I allow Tyler to put me through. Of course, I'm not victim-blaming, but I allow this to keep happening. Rather than take action to prevent him from hurting me, I keep letting him back in. An abuser is like a black hole; not only will you be sucked in before a blink of an eye, both a black hole and said abuser will leave you in a deep, dark, dangerous place where you just fade away.

I can only stand the sight of myself for a few moments before it makes me sick, especially with this busted lip. I step over the side of the tub, pull the curtain over and turn the water on. Hot water beating on my back after a day like today feels like absolute heaven. After dealing with Tyler and walking in that cold weather, not once, but twice, this shower is making me feel like a million bucks. Nolan has no conditioner, so I'd better pull my hair up and keep it dry. I wish I could stand under this hot water forever, but I feel it slowly becoming colder. Nolan probably thinks I got lost. I have been in the shower for at least twenty minutes, but hey, who's counting?

"Oh my God… there are no towels," I whisper to myself.

The second scariest thing in the world is taking a shower/bath at someone's home and not having towels. The first scariest thing in the world is when you use somebody's bathroom and the toilet won't flush – those are both equally embarrassing accounts. Wait, not having toilet paper to use is also on that list.

Note to self: please remember to always keep this mental list in mind, so I at least have tissues in my purse, if need be.

I can't just stand here expecting to dry off, I'll be here for half an hour.

Here goes nothing. I get out of the shower, turn the water off and crack open the door like half of a half of an inch and yell,

"Ummm, Nolan?

"Ummm, Aliza?"

Smartass.

"I hate to bother you, but there are no towels in here and I kind of need one to dry off," I state.

I hear him laughing.

"That sounds like an issue, doesn't it?" he jokes.

"Seriously, dude?"

"Hold on, I'm coming up with one now," he hands it to me through the crack of the door.

Finally, I'm dried off and dressed. I hang the towel up and walk downstairs to get my cigarettes out of my coat pocket. I should try to quit, considering I don't smoke a lot, unless I'm stressed out. Nicotine is addicting, however that isn't why people calm down when they are mad. The breathing technique is what calms a person down, inhaling and then exhaling. Not too many people realize this; they swear the nicotine and other shit helps, but it doesn't.

"Feeling better?" Nolan asks.

"For the most part. I'm exhausted and over today."

"I'm going to jump in the shower and smoke before I go to bed. I'll be done when I'm done. You can watch Netflix or whatever. You can even come chill upstairs if you want, instead of being down here by yourself."

"I might call Ally while you're in the shower. I'll be up when you're done," I tell him.

When I hear the bathroom door shut, I run upstairs to get my bag, I guess I have some crap to write about after a day like today. This bag is filled to the top. I don't care how wrinkled my clothes get, I toss them out, get my journal and my pen and then throw everything back in the bag. I was going to leave my phone in the bag, but I see all the texts and missed calls. Unfortunately, most are from Tyler with an assortment of texts and calls from Nolan earlier and Ally more recently. I don't have the strength to check these texts from anyone.

Entry #75

I'm single, thankfully. My day has been shit. I have a fat lip – oh and I was choked and hit with a lighter, which is more painful than it sounds. Currently, I can't really go home because my psycho ex is just waiting to "talk"; don't let that fool you, though. He really just wants to bully me into staying with him by using fear as his tool. You would be amazed at how well that works. I dealt with this for 3 years, but today, I am DONE! I am not doing it anymore. I don't have to. I know the worst part about me leaving him, in his eyes, is not being able to live free like he has been doing. He doesn't want to work, and I paid the bills. I took care of EVERYTHING.

In all honesty, I have no idea how I am actually going to get away from him. He doesn't take no for an answer, so I know he will be back one day. Whether he has to kick a door down or come through a window, I won't be able to lock him out of my apartment. I can always move out and go back home until he gets the point, but then my parents will learn that they were right about him and I can't let them know they were right. My pride is a monster, intent on destroying me. I do have to call them tomorrow and let them know I won't be home, indefinitely. And I do have work tomorrow...well, today, and thankfully I have a decent outfit in my bag and Nolan's place is closer to work than my house by 15 minutes.

*My phone will not stop going off and it is getting more annoying with every notification. I probably should check it, since it could be my parents or someone other than that psycho. It's my mom calling me, followed by 15... yes, **15** unread texts from Tyler. I'd better call her and see what she wants.*

Truly,

Miss Popular

First, I'll call my mother back, as she is more important than his crazy ass. I select her name to call and waited for an answer…

"Hello Aliza, what are you doing?" my mom asks.

"Nothing, why?"

She lets out a sign of relief. "Well, Tyler stopped by here to see if you came by. He said you guys had a disagreement and that you stormed out. Are you okay? What's going on?" she pries.

"I'm fine and yes, we did get into a little argument. I saw a message from someone saved under the name Maria and had some kind of intuition that there could be a possibility that she has other priorities than just being his friend," I explain carefully, in rather PG reasoning.

"What did it say? Is he seeing someone?"

"Honestly, Mom, I didn't get a chance to read the texts. I just saw a lot and that was enough for me. I'm not totally sure what is going on, but I figured I should take a breather tonight, so Ty and I can talk about it in a day or two."

Here we go with her theatrics.

"Suspicions are more than enough ground to make assumptions. If I knew that I would have told him right where to go when he came by. He acted very concerned, and that made me nervous. I should have known he did something tasteless. However, I'm not surprised," she goes on.

"Mom, it's not a big deal. I stopped over at Nolan's and we're waiting for Ally to come over to hang out, too. If Tyler tries to call you or stop by, just say you haven't talked to me. I don't need him coming over to Nolan's when I need time away from him, you know?"

"Don't you worry, I won't say a word! As a matter of fact, I won't answer a single text or call from that asshole!"

"Thanks, Mom. Try not to commit any mysterious murders in the meantime," I joke.

She laughs into the phone. "Since you're okay, I'm going to bed. I'm exhausted. Are you going to work in the morning? You have all that time saved up, so why not take a day off? If you're worried about money, I'll leave $60.00 on top of the refrigerator for you."

"That's a good idea, actually – I could use a break! It's not really the money, though. One day off won't kill me, but thank you. I'll call you tomorrow. I'm probably going to shut my phone off so he doesn't call or text it all night. I need some sleep, and I'm even going to try and sleep in. Goodnight," I say and wait for her to hang up.

"Goodnight. Enjoy time with your friends and not with that bastard," she says laughing, then hangs up.

Immediately, a text catches my attention.

"You aren't at your parents' and you aren't at Ally's, so that leaves me one more place to look. If you don't think, I'm coming there... think again.

My heart sinks and I quickly grab my journal, pen and cell phone, then race up the steps. I bang on the bathroom door in a panic.

"Nolan are you almost done? You need to come out here, PLEASE!" I yell.

"I mean, I am now! What the hell is going on?" he yells back through the door.

"Tyler said he is on his way here because he knows I'm not at my mom's or Ally's. You have to act like I'm not here. Please, let him in, act normal and I'll hide up here," I beg.

"If he's going to act that tough and come by here, I'm going to do more than just hide you. I'll probably punch him in his teeth, if you want the truth!"

"No, please. I can't deal with any more drama tonight. Can you please just do that for me?"

"So you're going to sit in a room and you want me let him in, so he thinks you aren't here? If that's the case, throw your bag on my closet shelf and you can sit in my room until he leaves," he says.

"Knowing him, he's going to try and look in every room, so I'm staying out of sight. You're dealing with a psycho, Nolan, one who doesn't give up."

Nolan looks at me with a smirk, not an "up to no good" smirk, either. It's the "I will kill somebody" kind of smirk. I can see his blood is boiling the more we talk about this. I run upstairs and throw my bag on the top shelf in his closet. You can barely see it because he has blankets and sheets clumped up there. Men are so messy!

I hear him come up the steps. He slowly creeps into his room and just stands against the doorway staring at me.

"What's wrong?" I ask, nervously.

"Besides you being so scared that you want me to hide you, nothing at all. I mean, this is pretty fucking aggravating that you're this scared. He deserves his ass beat, and I think me doing so is way overdue."

This is the first time that I think he's actually gotten mad at me, and it's making me uneasy, "Listen, I'm sorry. I'll stay at Ally's tomorrow, and then you won't have to get involved."

"You're kidding, right? I'm not mad at *you*. Why would you assume that? I'm mad because you are literally afraid of your own boyfriend…"

"Ex-boyfriend," I interrupt.

"Ex-boyfriend, my bad. Expecting me to just let him do this and walk into my house looking for you, while I'm looking at your fat lip, is making me want to kill him. I could never get mad at you for any of this and as far as I'm concerned, you're better off staying here with me." His voice gets louder.

He cares. He cares a lot. He cares more than I ever gave him credit for. I sit on his bed, wrapping my arms around my knees and dropping my head onto my lap in a defeated demeanor.

"I just want him to go away... forever..." I cry.

I cry. I cry because I'm scared. I cry because I was abused. I cry about being unable to go home, safely. I cry about Nolan being mad. I cry about having a friend who cares in the awkward way that he does.

"Aliza, he's not going to lay a hand on you because you are not going to be going home, and if you *really* need to go home, I will come with you," he reassures me.

"Thank you, Nol."

He scoots over and put his arm around my shoulders, "Just relax, alright? We'll take care of this," he says as he pulls my head towards his chest.

Thankfully, I stop crying. I could sit like this forever. If only that were possible. He rests his hand on the top of my head while we sit there in silence. Not a single word was said in those five minutes. Our breathing is in sync and that is the only sound in the room, until we hear a knock on the door. I jump up quickly and look at him for some kind of direction.

"Go hang out in the spare room, sit on the side of the bed and keep the door open. If he goes upstairs to use the bathroom, he'll be able to see right in the room. With the door being open, his stupid ass won't waste his time. Make sure your phone is on silent, not even vibrate, because if he finds you, I promise I will beat his ass," he says in an angry tone.

"Got it."

"This is the last time this happens. Next time, which I'm hoping there won't be a next time, I am going to knock him the hell out," he says.

I nod my head in understanding and quickly run into the spare room. I make sure my phone is on completely silent settings and slide it into my pocket. This is the most nerve-wracking thing I have ever endured. I hear the front door open and Tyler's voice makes my stomach turn, instantly. What has my life come to?

"What's going on, bro?" Nolan asks Tyler.

"Nothing, same shit with Aliza… always starting some bullshit. Have you talk to her at all?"

No surprise there – he's made me sound like the asshole as soon as he opened his mouth. He has a lying problem, a terrible lying problem! I think at times he believes his own lies, which makes it worse because he will fight you tooth and nail. There is nothing more annoying than knowing the truth, but being told it's a lie.

Nolan replies, "I actually talked to her about an hour or two ago. She said you guys got into a pretty bad argument and that she wasn't staying home tonight. I assumed she was with Ally or something."

"Nah, she's not with Ally. I stopped over there and Ally went nuts and told me to get the fuck off her property and that she hasn't heard from Aliza. She said if she hears that I hurt her again, shit is going to hit the fan. That bitch is crazy. As far as the hurting Aliza comment, that's some bullshit, too," Tyler lies some more.

"Liza said this argument got pretty physical. Did she really leave you over those texts and pictures? She said she did, but I didn't know if it was a heat of the moment break-up or for good."

"Who knows with her – she's another one who needs help. She starts up about nothing and all it does is screw this relationship up even more. If she's so concerned about me cheating, then maybe she should figure out what the fuck she did to push me to that point," Tyler says.

"Bro, I'm not trying to play sides, but how did she 'push' you to cheat? That doesn't make any sense. She does a lot for you and everybody else, so I'm kind of confused here." Nolan's voice starts growing louder.

The anger in Tyler's voice is also quickly increasing. "All you know is what Aliza tells you. That bitch is crazy and does nothing for me. She caused all these problems, and this is why our relationship is messed up."

"I don't know, dude. If I talk to her, I'll let her know you were looking here, and at Ally's too. Try her parents' house."

"I was already at her parents'. Her mom had no idea that she was even gone from our place. Can I use the bathroom before I go?" Tyler asks.

I hear Nolan say yes, then I hear Tyler trying to be quiet as he walks up the stairs. I can't help but get nervous. My breathing starts getting faster and it feels like a weight is on my chest… the anxiety from him being so close is killing me. I know him like an open book, so I shouldn't be surprised. He is so obsessed with catching me in the act of something, and I have no idea why. Maybe it is his own guilty conscience.

The bathroom door shuts, I hear him pee and then the toilet flushes. He is right in front of this bedroom and here I am laying against the opposite side of the bed, trying to hide. He needs to get the hell out of here before I go into a full-fledged panic attack! I heard the floorboards creak in front of Nolan's bedroom; he must be trying to look in there. What a psycho!

Tyler's voice startles me as he flies down the stairs. "Nolan, is there a reason Aliza's fucking sneakers were right in center view in your bedroom?"

"Oh shit. She must have left them here last night. She had a Victoria Secret's bag full of different clothes, shoes and make-up because we hung out with a couple friends last night, and her and Ally got ready here. Bring 'em home, I'm sure she is going to need them."

Oh my God, my damn shoes! Nolan is pretty convincing. There isn't a quiver in his tone. On the other hand, I'm not even sure I know how to breathe.

"Yeah, I probably will. I'm going to see if I can find her. If she calls you, which I'm sure she will, tell her I stopped by and want her to come home. She always fucking calls you," he said.

"No problem, bro. Good luck. I'm sure she's cool, just needs some time to chill out."

I am probably safe to run out of the spare bedroom when I hear the door shut, but I can't get up. My anxiety and fears have me pinned to the ground and my breathing is still heavy. Hearing Nolan walk up the steps isn't even convincing enough to get me up.

He walks in and turns the light on, "You owe me," Nolan asserts.

"I know I do… thank you so much. I almost stopped breathing when he said he found my sneakers. What the hell? I didn't forget to turn my phone off, I was able to remain quiet, you played it off so good and of course, BOOOM! My sneakers are in plain view."

"Just so you know, I can and never will do that ever again," he announces.

"Trust me, there won't be a next time. I am so done with him. The next month or so is going to be a little wacky though, because he isn't like normal people. He doesn't get the hint that it's over," I say as I shake my head in disbelief that this is my life.

He extends a hand out to help me up, which I really don't need, but I'll milk the situation for a minute. He pulls me up and we walk straight into his room. I walk over and pull my Vicky bag off the shelf and throw it on the ground. Thank God he didn't see that, or the whole cover would have been blown, since he saw me run down the street with the bag draped over my shoulder.

Rubbing my eyes, I look over at Nolan. "I'm exhausted. Throw me a pillow and a blanket to take into the spare room, please? With my luck, if I sleep on the couch, he'll see me through a window because he's a creep."

"Take whatever you need," he says.

I walk over to the closet, jump up and grab some sheets. I throw them on top of my bag and walk into the spare bedroom. I doubt that I'm going to sleep tonight, but I sure as hell am going to try. It helps that Nolan is here and Tyler has no access to me at all. Tyler is talking to another girl, so why is he so worried about Nolan and I talking? I have no idea who this Maria girl is. I have to do some investigating, because I'm dying to know who she is. Maria probably isn't even her real name.

CHAPTER 9

"I put my phone's passcode in and begin to type.

"STOP going door-to-door looking for me. Everyone is calling me, including my mom, and they're saying you were all at their houses! You got caught cheating and want to blame me for this fight... that makes no sense! You don't get to manipulate every shitty situation that you get yourself into, on top of physically hurting me and expecting me to come waltzing back. I AM DONE!"

I don't care if that was petty – he isn't the only one who can do what he wants to people. Plus, he isn't going to find me here and if he does, Nolan will handle it. For the first time in a while, I actually feel good about my life in a weird way. However, when I feel my phone vibrate, my stomach goes into knots.

"Don't fucking tell me what to do. You are a psycho with such bad trust issues and insecurities and no guy will deal with that shit! You'll be home eventually, you fucking idiot."

Does he not see where these trust issues stem from? I didn't just wake up one morning with them, and they don't stem from random insecurities. He needs to disappear because he will never go away.

All I want to do is sleep, but I know I won't be able to. My mom is right; I should take a day or two off. I never call out and I have the time to spare, so screw it. Debating if I should text Helen tonight or wake up early and call, I take a deep breath and a minute before texting that asshole back.

"Whatever you say. You need to face reality – you got caught cheating, I saw the texts and the pictures. There is NO way you can lie your way out of this. I am done being passive when it comes to the shit you put me through. I sure as shit do not deserve the abuse, either. Don't bother me again! I only texted you to inform you that we are done

and to stop going to my friends/family's houses looking for me. And get out of my place. Go worry about 'Maria'."

He can say all he wants back, but I am NOT answering him.

"Go screw," I say while tossing my phone to the other side of the bed.

I take my journal out and contemplate writing or not. I have nothing else to do. I'm not sure if Nolan is awake and I don't want to go into his bedroom if he is still sleeping. With my luck, the second I walk in there, he will wake up and it will look like I'm being a creep. I grab my journal, feel around the bottom of the bag for my pen and decide to grab my phone so I can put some music on. I need an outlet. Since murder is illegal and pouring my heart out to Nolan is not an option right now, writing will have to do.

Entry #76

Psycho decided to stop at my mom's house, Ally's house and Nolan's house, but I sat in the spare bedroom and made Nolan play it off like I wasn't here. I know that sounds like a stupid thing to do, but Ty isn't going to give up, so I had to do it. I owe Nolan big-time because I know how incredibly hard that was. I hate swallowing my pride, so expecting him to swallow his pride because I don't like swallowing mine is a lot to ask.

Considering I just left my boyfriend of almost four years today, you would think I would be sad. That's the farthest thing from the truth, though. I feel relieved and I also have a ton of *anxiety because I am afraid. I have no idea what he is going to do, but he **WILL** do something, and merely knowing that fact is enough to make me want to rip my hair out. Constantly feeling scared of somebody who I am supposed to love and feel safe with – that takes so much out of a person.*

The weird thing about all of this is that I'm listening to songs that remind me of Nolan or songs that we listened to together. Oddly enough, I decided to throw some Incubus on and there is something about all of these songs that throws me into this zone of calming and reflection. Thoughts that leads to a lot of regret, and it actually gives me the balls for the duration of the song to want to go talk to Nol and pour my pathetic fucking heart out.

The fact that "Stellar" is playing and he is only a few feet away makes me want to run into his room, get high, get lost and just tell him everything. I won't, though, because of these invisible boundaries that we think we both created for the other person.

I might sound like an idiot, but I can put certain music on and I just feel as if my mind goes to this parallel universe; I seriously get lost in my thoughts. It's a universe where I actually feel at ease. It's this place in my mind where I go to when I want to imagine my life as something good. Nolan is always there; we're together, we're drunk, we're actually feeling good. This is a place where I actually feel comfortable, and it all stems from what we use to have. I just miss that new, daring, lustful feeling; it's something I haven't felt in years.

This is bullshit that I just started crying. Why can't I say all of this to him like I'm saying it to you... well, writing it. I feel like the last couple years with Ty have broken me down into nothing. I am numb, I'm delusional and I need to actually feel like someone wants me for me. This front that I keep putting on is killing me more and more every single fucking day. I am so defeated that I don't think I can ever win at anything.

All I want to do is feel something. I want to feel wanted. I want to feel loved. I want to feel safe. I want to feel worth it. I once enjoyed life. My life was this parallel universe that I keep wishing I can go back to. My past is a parallel universe that I want to both escape and take the good parts from and make something new with them.

I cannot keep writing because I am going to wake him up with my crying.

Truly,

Broken and bruised

I shut my journal, put on "Champagne Supernova" and lay my head against the wall. I am at my breaking point; I have hit rock-bottom. Rock-bottom doesn't have a certain time or place, unfortunately. I am crying so hard that it hurts to even open my eyes. I tuck my head in between my knees and just cry. As a little girls, we dream of weddings and babies and husbands. We don't dream of abusive men or dead-end jobs, or shitty, dilapidated apartments. I am living in every way I never wanted to and it finally broke me. I am crying on my best friend's floor, in his spare bedroom. And I have a crazy ex-boyfriend actually searching for me, so that he can bring me home and beat the shit out of me all because he got caught cheating. Am I cursed, or is this some kind of punishment for something I did?

My heart pauses, as I pick my head up, startled. I'm so lost in this web of fucking disaster, but something touches me. There is a hand on my head.

"What's wrong? Are you okay?" Nolan asks, his voice shaking.

"No…"

I lose it even more, I bury my head in his chest and let it all out again. He's going to think I'm a crazy, unstable mess at this point. Before I can even say a word, he picks me up and sits me on his bed.

"Listen to me," he says with urgency.

I pick my head up and look at him.

"You are okay. You have no reason to be crying over some scumbag who beats you. You're safer here than you are anywhere else."

"I'm not just crying over him, Nolan. I don't give a shit that he was cheating on me. I wished for months that I could find a reason to leave him, which makes no sense because putting his hands on me should have been enough, but it wasn't," I continue through the tears.

"Well, then what's wrong?"

"Nothing! I don't fucking know," I say while trying to walk away.

"No, you're not doing this. If you don't want to talk about it that's cool, but just relax. Lay down."

I start to slowly get up and walk back into the spare bedroom when I see him turn around and move his pillows and blankets.

"Stay in here, if you want," he says.

"Wait, are you sure? Where are you going to sleep?" I ask.

"What do you mean? I'm going to sleep right there ... in my bed," he points towards the left side.

I don't say a word. I take my headphones out of my phone, wrap them up and then toss them onto his dresser. Within seconds I feel so nervous, like when your stomach feels all weird and you start to get clammy hands. What is this?! I'm acting like a twelve-year-old who has just seen her crush at school. I'm a mess. I sit on the side of the bed and push myself against the wall. As I pull the blankets over my legs, he follows suit.

I notice his head turn towards me, with his back against the wall. "What?" I ask, laughing a little.

"Nothing at all," he says. "I didn't think the day would come around again where I got you into my bed," he jokes.

"Yeah, well enjoy it while it lasts."

All of a sudden we're both propped against the wall giggling like idiots. This is why I feel the way I do about him. Life with him is easy; I'm at ease whenever we hang out. Of course it hasn't been like this in a few years, but in a way it feels like it has *always* been like this, like nothing has changed. I don't think we will ever get all of that back, whatever "that" was, because I don't think he wants to be held down and I'm sorry, I'm not fifteen years old anymore. If I'm with somebody, it is official, and it isn't this friends with benefits, come-and-go arrangement.

"You know, I'm really not upset that Tyler and I broke up. I have been wishing to get the strength to do this for a long time now. It just sucks that I am afraid to be in my own apartment, because I don't know what he is going to do," I say to Nolan.

He takes a drag off of a blunt and looks back at me, "You're not going home, so there is nothing to worry about. Just stay here for a while. You can be my new roommate."

"Okay, but then after 'a while' is up, what happens? If I'm paying for my apartment, I want to live in it at least."

I have no idea what he is getting at. He's high, so I am almost positive that it has something to do with this.

"A little while isn't going to be up. Stay here as long as you want."

"So when you get a girlfriend, you think she will find this normal? I definitely wouldn't," I prod, laughing.

"I won't need a girlfriend if you're living here…"

The moment my brain processes that comment, I probably give him the most awkward look imaginable. Before I have a chance to say a word, he grabs my face and kisses me. I stop breathing, but I don't stop kissing him. I keep my eyes shut because I know his aren't shut; they never are. I come up for air and pull back to look at him. Not a word needs to be said. I lean back in and start to kiss him again. In sudden haste, we are laid out on the bed, breathing each other in without taking our lips off one another. I don't have a single interest in stopping this, so I hope he doesn't, either. I quickly pull back, grab my lighter out of my hoodie pocket, lean over him and snatch the butted half of a blunt in his ashtray.

He props himself up and looks at me, confused.

"Seriously?" he asks.

"Yeah, seriously," I hand it to him after taking a pull.

He takes two fast and long pulls, holds it in for a few seconds and then exhales. He tries to hand it to me, and then I remember that I need to at least text Helen and let her know that I won't be in tomorrow. I run over, grab my phone, and send her a text saying that I'm feeling good and I need the day off, then throw the phone on the floor and grab the blunt. I take another long pull and hand it back to him. There he goes, giving me that smirk that I have grown to love. He exhales what he has in his throat, tosses it in the ashtray and grabs my face again.

The high kicks in and I am lost. We kiss for at least ten minutes, then he works his way down to my neck. I run my hand through his hair and start to pull his shirt over his head. It's like we are on a time limit, as if we have to do this as quickly as possible. We are undressed within seconds and I can guarantee that we broke a world record or at least came pretty damn close. That's the end of that. What I have been missing for the last couple years was all of him and this disastrous, messy, lustful feeling. We throw each other around the bed for about forty-five minutes, taking turns on top, kissing each other, barely breathing. I haven't felt this way in a very long time and although this is nothing new, he still makes me feel like he did when we started messing around.

When we were done, we lay there in silence. His head is on my thigh and I just keep running my fingers through his hair, slowly.

I finally catch my breath, but my heart is going so fast that it's kind of embarrassing.

He picks his head up and looks at me. "Don't die on me now, Jesus," he says.

"Shut up. Give me a cigarette." I can barely speak.

He leans over to the bedside table and grabs one cigarette and his lighter. He cocks his head to the side and lights his cigarette in the sexiest way possible. I know smoking is not cute, but there is just something about how he lights them after we have sex. He always has that smirk and this satisfied look on his face. I reached off the bed to get my phone so I can see if Helen responded back.

I hate calling out. I get anxiety from it, even though I haven't done it in forever. Luckily, she didn't answer. I throw the phone back onto the floor, and reach for my thong to put it back on. I stand up, put it on and grab his cigarette. Normal people would think this silence is weird, but it isn't at all for us. I love the silence after sex, the tired, happy, euphoric feeling I experience.

"Here, take this cigarette, finish it. I'm running to the bathroom," I tell him.

He takes the cigarette, puts his boxers on and climbs into bed. Rule of thumb, always pee after sex – you'll thank me later for these important hygiene tips. Right before I turn the light off, I catch a glimpse of myself in the mirror and for the first time in a while, I feel and look like myself. I give the mirror a faint smile, flip my reflection off and walk into Nolan's room. I climb into bed and for the first time in my life, he puts his arm around me and we we're falling asleep together. Never have we ever slept in the same bed. I get comfortable and drift into my dreams with a smile.

CHAPTER 10

I hear my phone ringing and instantly wake up. Shit, I should have tried to call Helen. I grab my phone and thank God it's only seven in the morning. I check my texts and she said she "hopes I feel better". I text her back and tell her to update me during the day about Corporate's findings. I walk into the spare bedroom to get my bag, and my phone's at like eight percent battery. I return to the room, plug my phone in and climb back into bed. Once I get comfortable, Nolan throws his arm around me and pulls me over to his side of the bed. At this moment, I don't think I will ever stop loving him, regardless of how this turns out.

Saddened by the thought of us not being together, I can't fall asleep. So many things are running through my mind, like am I literally nothing more than a piece of ass? Could I ever be more than that to him?

An hour goes by and finally he starts to wake up. I wish I fell back asleep, but seeing him look over at me while being half asleep, smiling, kind of warms my ice-cold heart.

"I was thinking I was waking up and you were going to be gone," he says, laughing.

"Considering I'm sort of homeless, not today."

"I'm supposed to go look at a car later. Do you want to come with me? Jason is giving me a ride."

"Yeah, that's fine. What time are we going?" I ask.

"I don't know, he said to call him when I get up. So let's say in about an hour or two."

"In the meantime I'm going to make a grocery list for a few things."

"That's a good idea. I don't think I ever did that before.," he says.

"I can tell by all the pizza boxes I've seen. I'm about to jump in the shower and get your filth from last night off of me," I say jokingly.

"Stop playing and acting like that was my fault."

I look at him with the most serious look and he starts laughing. He knows that was him. I have to talk to him tonight because either this becomes official, or this becomes nothing at all. Moving on is essential – having time to find yourself is essential too – but when you have felt this much of a connection with somebody… you don't need time because I have had that time. I don't care who has an issue with moving on fast. Just because Tyler and I have been physically together, there hasn't been any connection. It has been more of a nightmare rather than a relationship.

I close the bathroom door behind me, undress and hop under the hot water. It's like a total 360 from last night. I feel relaxed and better all around. It's weird how the presence of somebody special can change every aspect of a person and their demeanor. We are always told that happiness comes from within and we can't be happy with another person if we are not happy with ourselves first, but I disagree. Maybe it is my codependent ways and attitude, but I feel that we all deserve somebody to make us feel happy. After dealing with an abusive life, it's nice to have someone make you feel good. I think we all need to have somebody help build us up, particularly after someone has stripped us of everything good we once thought about ourselves.

"What the fuu…" I turned around scared, and almost cracked Nolan.

"You either got to hurry up or I'm jumping. Jay got called into work, so we have to get there and get this done. I think this car is good, so I have to get the title and tag."

"Man, I'm trying. I just jumped in."

I don't really know why he gives me ultimatums, because he jumps in anyways.

"You know when I jump in the shower, that's my time?" I let him know.

"Yeah, well we don't have time for 'your time'."

Laughing, I turn the hot water off and jump out real quick.

"Ohhh you have jokes now, okay," he says.

I run into the room, dry off quick and get dressed. He's sneaky, so he will get back at me. I have to watch my back now. Thank God I still have my straightener and curling iron in my bag. I plug my straightener in and sit it on top of the dresser.

I peek my head out of the doorway. "Nolan, do I have time to dry and straighten my hair?"

"I guess. He said he will be here in an hour," he yells across the hallway.

I wrap the towel around my head and put some make-up on. I'm dreading the idea of going home, but luckily I am coming back here. I unlock my phone to see if I have any missed calls or texts; of course I do. I have a missed call from Psycho and two texts from Helen. I open my inbox to see what she has to say.

"Good news, Aliza. We did really well this time and there are hardly any tags. Nursing has a few, but not a lot. Are you feeling better? I am going to mark today as a paid day off, which leaves you with eighty-two hours, after eight have been deducted."

I should use my PTO; after all, I worked hard for that. Every year I always let some time expire because honestly, what do I need to take off for? It wasn't like Tyler and I go out or took vacations.

"Awesome, that's a relief! Thank you, I appreciate it. I think I came down with a little virus. If you could mark tomorrow as a PTO too, I'd really appreciate it."

Screw the missed calls. I am not letting that asshole ruin my day today. I straighten my hair kind of fast and pulled it into a high pony. I look pretty decent today and I actually feel happy, most likely because of last night, but that doesn't matter.

I walk down the steps and yell into the other room, "Nolan, when are we leaving? I'm ready."

"Cool, he's going to be here within the next fifteen to twenty minutes."

"What kind of car are you looking at?" I ask.

"It's a black Audi. It's nice and fast," he says excitedly.

I start to laugh. "Great… all you need is something fast," I tease.

I open the refrigerator to get the iced tea. I grab two glasses from the cabinet and fill them. Nolan is on the phone, so I quietly hand them to him.

Looking annoyed, he hangs up the phone and looks at me. "Here's the thing, Tyler was at Jason's last night, and so I don't know if you want to come for this ride or not, being that Jay may possibly tell Tyler you're with me. It's your call, Liza. It doesn't matter to me."

"Of course. I'd rather wait here until you get home. I don't even want to deal with the extra drama because Jay has a big mouth. The second he drops us off to get your car, you know he will call Tyler," I say, extremely pissed off.

Nolan walks over to where I am standing, puts his phone down and kisses me on the forehead, "Listen, I'll be as fast as I can. It shouldn't take that long anyways. I have the exact amount that I need for the car and I have the money to transfer everything. I doubt I'll be gone longer than two hours. Just hang out here and if you get bored, text me. Lock the door once I leave, and go chill in my bedroom," he says.

I nod my head in agreement and follow him to the front door. "I'll see you in a little bit," I wave him off.

Just like the master said, I lock the doors, get my glass and go into his bedroom. I don't know why I'm aggravated that he is gone, but I do enjoy laying in his bed. I don't need the TV on, I can just lay here and enjoy the silence until he comes back. I lean over the bed and pull my journal out of my bag. I have some updating to do in this thing… good updates, for once.

Entry #77

Last night wasn't what I expected. I thought I'd be sleeping alone in the spare bedroom. Nope, was I was wrong. During my mental breakdown, Nolan carried me to his bedroom and told me that I could sleep in there. I wasn't going to refuse. Obviously we did more than sleep, which I needed more than anything. It's weird, because I told myself unless I knew there weren't going to be any games, I'd never give in to the temptation of sleeping with him. However, last night was different. It wasn't just this lustful thing; I actually feel like he cared, and now I know he did and still does.

Unfortunately, he needed Jay to give him a ride to get his new car and since Jay was with Tyler last night, I stayed home. Jason has a big mouth and loves to cause drama, as if he's a popular teenage girl. As a result, I have to hide out here. Nolan didn't give a shit if I came or not, but I knew it wasn't a good idea. I had a few missed calls from Tyler last night, and I never called him back. Should I text him and see what he wanted? I'm sure it's some bullshit, like always!

I have never felt stronger than I do today. I know that I am officially done with Tyler and that abusive relationship. I have hope that Nolan and I can try to be that one thing we never were. In my mind, I feel like I am setting myself up for failure, but what else do I have to lose? I pay my own way, I have my own place, so I don't need anyone to keep me going. However, it's nice to have someone in my life for other reasons, especially having been head over heels in love with them for years. When you have such a strong chemistry with another person, that is something that isn't irreplaceable.

Regardless what happens, I have to face that asshole so he understands that it is OVER. There is no reading in-between the lines, no gray areas, nothing. I am done. I still have a while before Nolan comes home. I need a nap, I am seriously mentally stressed.

I think sleep is the only thing that will help me at this point. I mean, I guess alcohol is always an option, too.

Truly,

Mentally Exhausted

CHAPTER 11

I wake up to Nolan shaking my arm.

"Come outside and check my car out!" he's yelling excitedly.

"Oh my God, give me a second, I'm literally just waking up…"

"You have like five minutes to come check this out, or I'm going to carry you outside," he says as he walks down the steps.

I throw my UGGs and coat on as I walk to the front door. I feel my phone vibrate and as I pull it out of my hoodie pocket, seeing the "T" is enough for me to let it go. Tyler needs to go the hell away already. I open the door and Nolan is sitting on the hood of his black Audi while smoking a cigarette. His grin stretches from ear to ear, and seeing that makes my smile spread just as wide.

"Wow! This so nice, Nol... I love this." I try to match my excitement to his. I could give a shit about the car, but his excitement is what's making me happy.

He flicks his cigarette butt to the curb and opens the driver's side door. "Let's go," he says.

"Wait, do you have an aux cord?" I ask, climbing in. "We need some tunes."

"Shit... no..."

I open the passenger side door and start to get out. "Hold on, I have one in my bag upstairs."

As I shut the car door and turn around to go inside, a figure down the street catches my eye. This man – I think it's a man – is way down the street, but as soon as I see him, my stomach drops. Shit! That is definitely Ty. I run into the house, grab the aux cord and run back into the car. I throw Nolan the cord and try to discreetly look out the side mirror and the review mirror without him noticing. I can see the figure getting closer, yet he still has a bit to go.

"Nolan, can we just go, please? Tyler is at the end of the street, and I know he saw me," I tell him nervously.

"What the fuck? He's actually stalking you in broad daylight?"

I turn to look out the back window and there he is. He doesn't care if we see him. He is purposely doing this so that we know that he caught us. In a daze, I feel the car jerk and Nolan speeds off. I guess you could say the sound of his tires peeling on the hot asphalt is what brought me back to life.

"Aliza, not only am I saying this because he is being stupid by creeping around my place, but do you see how fucked-up this stalking thing is? I can't always be with you, which means you have to do something to get him to back the hell off," he says, his voice growing louder with every word he speaks.

I keep my eyes on the road in front of us. "Do you think I don't know this? This isn't anything new, Nolan. It's been like this for a long time now. Are you finally deciding to care, now that I'm back to being on-call when you need to get laid?" Wow, I shouldn't have said that. Why did I just say that?

"Do you honestly think I let you sleep over my house because I needed to get *laid*? You're kidding me, right? I told you to stay at my house so I don't have to see you with another fat lip or his finger-shaped bruises around your neck. Because no matter how much you really think you can hide them by leaving your hair down… I don't fucking miss any of it! If I was so desperate for a piece of ass, I could have called any bitch over to my house. Don't think for a second that I only have you to fall back on!"

I rip my aux cord out of his stereo. I'm not about to argue with him. Everything was going so great until this moment. I am not going to attempt to ruin this. I shouldn't have said what I said, but I feel like he always kept a blind eye to all of it. I am not a psychic. This is, and always has been, the biggest problem between Nolan and me: a lack of communication. The invisible boundaries that we act like we've set for each other need to come down.

"Let me out," I demand.

"You're crazy. I'm not letting you out with Psycho just a couple blocks away. Although you think I don't give a shit about you, I do," he snaps.

I feel the anxiety and regret building up in my chest. "Then bring me to my house. I need to get my stuff, anyway. I'll call Ally and have her pick me up, then I'll get my bag from your house."

"What is wrong with you? Aliza, just stop it and I'll come with you. We can get your stuff and go back to my place," he pleads with me.

"Nolan, just bring me home, please."

Not another word is said. We sit in silence for the whole ride to my house from that point on. He doesn't even turn the radio on, which is almost an impossible thing for him not to do. This is not how I wanted this shit to go, but it did. I should apologize and just get my stuff and return to his place, but I'm not going to. I need to clear my head. I thought getting things sorted out or started with him would help me. Maybe I was wrong. I might need to remain single and figure myself out before I figure myself out with another person added into my fucked-up life. He pulls in front of my apartment so that I can get out.

"Are you sure you don't want me come in with you, or wait here?" he asks.

"I'm good."

Without looking back, I shut the car door and continue into my apartment. Tyler had better not be here, but I'm sure he is. I stand at the top of the steps for a couple of seconds before I unlock the door. I need to get myself together, think of what I need and leave. I think I might be able to make it out of here before Tyler gets here. I pull my cigarettes out of my pocket and light one off of the stove. I am always losing lighters. I walk into my room, go through my drawers and grab a handful of underwear, bras, and socks and throw them in backpack. As I scour my closet, I pick out jeans, hoodies and a few nice tops. Next, I need to get my yoga pants and some t-shirts. I can't live without yoga pants. Then I hear the front door open. FUCK! I run over to the dirty clothes hamper and begin to throw some of those clothes out to sort them. If Tyler asks, I'll just say that I'm getting a load of laundry done. I have to do my laundry at my parents' anyways, so that will explain the backpack of clothes.

"Where's your boyfriend?' Tyler asks sarcastically.

Considering the events of the last two days, he has a large amount of pent-up anger. I cannot afford to have an argument because I am going to get my ass beat. I look up and play stupid. "What are you talking about?" I reply.

"Don't act like you didn't see me down the street from Nolan's house. Is that where you stayed? Did your little boyfriend Nolan hide you?" he starts screaming.

I throw the basket to the left of me and stand up. "Ty, I am not doing this. Let me get my shit. Leave me alone, and get away from me. Until you learn how to talk, rather than scream at me, we are not discussing anything. Go!"

Before I know it, he's started walking towards me. I try to push my way into the living room with my backpack on my back, and he pulls on it.

"Let me go!" I yell.

"Why? So you can go screw Nolan, while I'm spending my night looking for you?"

All of a sudden my front door slams shut…

"Tyler. Chill, man. Aliza, get your shit and let's go," Nolan commands.

Tyler lets go of me and of course he has to jerk me to the side. This is not going to be good. I run into my bathroom and grab my shampoo, conditioner and hairspray. That's when it all happens.

"Bro, don't walk into my place with an attitude. Aliza, if you really leave with him, you're fucked. I'm warning you now," Tyler says with an evil smile.

"This is why she left you. You think it's okay to beat up on women. Fight me instead." Nolan gets in his face.

From that second it's all over. Tyler puts his hands on Nolan's chest and pushes him towards the bedroom door. Then all of a sudden Nolan cocks his arm back and punches him in the face.

"Guys, stop, please!" I scream. "Nolan, let's go… come on!"

They throw each other onto the floor, into the walls and just keep hitting one another. I try to pull them apart and Tyler swings and hits me in the side. I go down like a ton of bricks. It takes a couple of seconds before I realize that he knocked the wind out of me. I get up again and jump in between them.

"Nolan, let's fucking go now… please," I beg.

Tyler takes a step back and mumbles something to Nolan. He then turns to me, his nostrils flaring and his eyes turning red. "You leave with him and you are done. Do you hear that, Nolan? You'd better stay with her every second of every fucking day because she's going to need you," he tells us in a calm manner.

"Go screw yourself, bro. If you think she's going to continue to get the shit kicked out of her from a low-life like you, you have another thing coming," Nolan says while grabbing my hand and pulling me down the steps. Finally, he slams the door behind us and we continue out of the house. The only sound we could hear was stuff being smashed and thrown around in my apartment and the two of us breathing heavily.

Once we get in the car, the tears start pouring from my eyes. I usually don't cry a lot and anyone will second that statement, but the last few days have been too much for me to bear. Nolan starts the car, but before driving away, he leans in and gives me a hug.

"Aliza, chill, okay? It's fine. He really isn't going to do shit anymore. I'm not going to let him," Nolan says quietly.

In between breaths, I try to speak as many words as I can, "I'm sorry… I didn't mean to drag you into this," I say, my voice barely audible.

"You don't have to be sorry."

He lets me go and drives off. I finally calm down after a couple minutes, thank God. He turns the radio on and puts his usual rap music on, which proves oddly comforting.

"Is this what you call music?" I joke.

He smiles and looks over quickly. "I just saved your life, let me jam."

"I guess you're right."

He turns his radio up and I hit him on his arm, laughing. Actually, he deserves an apology from earlier. I don't apologize often, so I'm debating if I should wait until we get home or not. He might just crash the car in shock when I say that I'm sorry.

I inhale deeply. "Nolan, I'm sorry for earlier. Obviously I know that you care about me and always did care. I was just aggravated and upset that this is what my life has turned into: pure chaos. I guess I just let Tyler convince me that you literally only even messed around with me because all I am, or was, is a piece of ass." I exhale.

He backs the car into his parking spot. "Well, I don't know why you would let that asshole make you believe anything. I also don't really know what you expected from me. You're hard-headed and you don't like to listen. After so long, what more was I going to say to get you to understand your relationship with him wasn't okay?" he says.

"I get it. There is only so much you could say at that point before it got me aggravated… same thing with Ally. Now I know that you guys were just looking out for me as much as you could."

He hands me half of his cigarette. "Are you done with him?" Nolan asks, looking into my eyes.

"Are you seriously asking me that? Yes, obviously," I say sarcastically.

"Aliza, I'm serious. I want to at least try to attempt us being together, but after all these years, I have no idea what I was or what I am to you. I mean, I don't hate us being friends, but it's not the most normal friendship, either," he admits.

"Wait, you want us to be together?"

He shuts his car door and walks over to mine.

"Did I stutter?"

"No, but I'm just surprised. I never thought this would ever happen."

"We have to chill and not rush into it, but I don't see why it can't happen. You know our friendship in the past was rocky, but we were too young and dumb to admit anything," he chuckles.

He unlocks his door and we walk in, threw everything on the floor and go into the kitchen. I sit down on the countertop and he comes over and wraps his arms around my waist. It feels good that we are on the same page for once in our whole entire lives of knowing one another. Without a word, I put my arms around his neck and just rest my cheek on his shoulder. We sit like that for about ten minutes until his phone starts ringing. He goes into his pocket and pulls it out. I catch a glimpse of the phone and see that Jay is calling him. He answers it and I jump off the counter to grab a drink. When I put the gallon of soda back in the refrigerator, he taps on the freezer and signals that he will be done in a minute. I'm dying to hear their conversation, but I decide to go sit on the couch and text Ally about everything that has happened.

"So Tyler already called Jay and probably everyone else he knows, because Jay said

Shawn was with Ryan, and Tyler called him too," Nolan sighs as he sits down next to me.

"You and Ryan still aren't getting along, are you?" I ask.

"Nope. That's probably why Tyler called him. Shawn was telling Jay that Ty and Ryan are going to be plotting some stupid shit against me the next time they see me alone or with you. You know they have to jump me because they are pussies," Nolan says.

"There's no reason for this at all. He's going to start all of this shit because I left him. I left him because I got fed up with the lies, abuse and all of it, so how am *I* the bad guy in all of this?" It's a rhetorical question.

"Liza, I could give a shit what Tyler and his minions have planned. They're a bunch of idiots."

I laugh. "Minions?" I repeat.

He laughs with me and then grabs my legs and throws them over him, so I am laying across him.

"Shut up. It was the first word that came to mind. I'm jumping in the shower quick, alright?" he says.

He throws my legs of off of him and we both walk up the steps as he disappears into the bathroom and I go into his bedroom. Ally hasn't answered me yet and I need to share this good news with somebody, so I pull my journal out of my bag and start to write.

CHAPTER 12

Entry #78

Yeah, I'm back again. Besides Asshole almost having the opportunity to kill me, then Nolan and Ty getting into a fist-fight in my living room, I do have some good news! Nolan actually does care and always did care. I let Tyler brainwash me into doubting what I meant to Nolan. We came to a conclusion that we should try and see how a relationship would work for us. Like Nolan said, our friendship is complex and ridiculous and in the past we were basically in a relationship – a weird one that neither of us confirmed, but it was a relationship, nonetheless. Okay, that sounds really confusing, but you get it. I'm sure I have said other things that could make someone's head spin way worse.

The only thing that I am kind of worried about now is the fact that Tyler will stop at nothing to hurt me, and now he is rounding his army of "minions" up, as Nolan calls them. I think Tyler is going to try and have people go after Nolan. I never meant for any of this to get bad, but Ty has a way of turning everything into chaos and destruction. Nolan can hold his own, better than Ty, but nobody can take on multiple people and win. I don't want him to get hurt. It's going to be a long couple of weeks, hopefully not months, until Tyler backs off.

I can't wait to lay down. I'm exhausted in every which way – not to mention, I could get used to sleeping next to someone who I actually want around me.

Truly,

Halfway to happiness

I hear the shower turn off, so I put my journal back into my duffel bag. I ran downstairs to bring my backpack upstairs, so I can empty it and see what I grabbed. I went into my apartment so fast that I wasn't really paying attention to what I took with me. Luckily, everything I picked is pretty versatile and I can make a couple outfits out of them. I still have yet to figure out how I am going to make Tyler leave that apartment. I hate calling the cops – that's just something you should try to avoid. Maybe I can talk to my landlord about having me sign a new lease without Tyler. Our lease was up two years ago and none of us thought to sign a new one. I fold everything that I keep in drawers and begin to put them back in my bag. Whether Nolan likes it or not, I have to hang some clothes up in his closet, most definitely my jeans to start.

I hear him walk into the bedroom. "Hey bud, do you have any hangers? I need to hang up a few outfits I grabbed, and my jeans."

"Yes I do." He bends down and pulls a whole pile of hangers out from under his bed.

"Thank ya," I say with a smile.

While he gets dried off and dressed, I work on getting all my clothes hung and out of the way. I clean my bags out and throw my make-up and hair products on top of his dresser. As I walk into the bathroom to store my shampoo and conditioner in there, he walks in behind me with my make-up, straightener and curling iron.

"You can keep these in the bathroom. After all, that's where you get ready anyway," he says.

"Good point. I just wasn't sure if you wanted anyone to see all my shit out in the open."

"You need to get out of this state of mind that I have some ulterior agenda. I told you that I want to give this a try. I'm not going to hide you, or anything that you bring to my house. If someone doesn't like the idea of me being with you, then they can go screw," he says, maintaining eye contact the whole time.

"I know, I'm sorry… I don't think you have other motives. I just have to get used to the idea of actually being with someone who wants to be with me. I mean, being with someone who I actually love… love to be with," I quickly shut my mouth because I almost said I loved him.

"That's another thing – stop always apologizing. If I hear you say sorry one more time for something that usually doesn't require an apology, just wait to see what happens to your sorry ass." He smiles and walks away.

I shut the bathroom door and hop in the shower. This all seems too good to be true. Of course the drama with Tyler isn't anything good, but I'm so used to his antics. I hope he cuts it out because I am afraid he might take this too far. I can't control him. If I could, we wouldn't be where we are today. There are so many changes happening in my life right now, and I have to take everything a day at a time.

I pull my hair into a bun so it won't get wet. I took a shower this morning and I really don't feel like drying and straightening my hair again. Oh, and I really need to get normal body wash here. It seems like I have a lot to do. Maybe it's too early for this, but I have no idea how Nolan and I are going to maintain a relationship when we both have our own places. I have always been an independent person, on paper at least. I always take care of own my finances since I have been on my own, plus everything in my apartment is mine. Tyler owns clothes and he bought me a laptop that he always says is his. Even if we were to figure out who is moving out of their place, what would we both do with our stuff? I have a fully-furnished apartment. Nolan could use some more furniture in this place, which would be an easy fix, but I don't know how I feel about moving out of my apartment that's near my parents. There is no reason for me to even think about all of this, considering the bullshit I already have on my plate.

I step out of the shower and look around for a towel. "Shit, Nolan left the towel in the bedroom," I say to myself.

"NOLANNNN," I yell through a closed door, because it's going to be too cold if I run into the bedroom.

"What's up?" he peeks into the bathroom.

"I think you left the towel in your bedroom. Can you get it for me?"

"Nah, I'd rather let ya air-dry," he says as he closes the door behind him.

Within a few seconds he comes in the bathroom with the towel and shuts the door behind him. I'm kind of confused as to why he's in here while I dry off, but I guess I can act like I don't even notice.

He sits on the back of the toilet and watches me wrap the towel around myself, through the mirror. "Do you have work tomorrow?" he asks.

"Actually, I took today and tomorrow off. I have a little under 80 hours of PTO time that I can use. Why, what's up?"

"I was thinking we could do something tomorrow. I didn't really figure anything out, but after the last 48 hours of your life, I thought you could use a distraction."

I brush my hair and then walk out of the bathroom. "I'm down for anything. Plan it and I'm on board," I say, smiling.

He walks over to me once I get dressed and throws me over his shoulders, then onto the bed.

"Seriously?" I try to get up and he pins me down to attempt to tickle me.

"Wait, I'm pretty sure you owe me for saving your life or something, right?" He gives me that smirk.

"Oh, so I have to repay you for every good deed you decide to do on your own?" I ask.

He grabs my arm and pulls me down next to him and in between kisses he says, "Something like that."

It doesn't take much for me to melt when he gets intimate. I have never been this easy for anybody and in return people, always acted like I was stuck-up. When it comes to

Nolan, I have no walls, no strength or anything – I cave instantly. He continues to kiss me on my neck, even when I am taking his shirt off. He gets my pants off, I get his pants off and that's the end of that. He flips me onto my back and I am done. I melt into him and my mind goes blank. I start to kiss his neck, then push him off of me. I grab his face and continue to kiss him as he lets me get on top. When this happens, time stands still. We both are perfectly in sync, from movements to breathing, and then he starts to go faster. The half-hour of us pacing ourselves turns into ten minutes full of a desperate need to get off. My hands grab the sheets and mattress so I can anchor myself down, and once I feel the goosebumps on his skin, I run my nails down his back and he is done. For five minutes we just lay there, trying to catch our breaths and slow our heartbeats down.

I roll over to the side of him and he turns towards me. "Are we even now?" I ask.

He smiles and says, "For now."

Out of nowhere my phone begins to ring and it startles me. I jump off the bed and run over to pick it up off the dresser.

"It's just my mom. Stay quiet, and I'll put it on speaker," I say before I answer.

"Hey, Mom…"

"What's going on with you and Tyler? He called us saying you were still missing."

"I was there today, but I'm at Nolan's now. Tyler and I broke up and I need time away from him because he can't accept that I caught him cheating… He left his cell phone on the counter when he was sleeping and it kept going off, so I looked at it. When I looked through the texts with that girl there were pictures of her boobs and everything."

"Aliza, I told you a long time ago that he was no good. I'm not throwing the I-told-you-so thing in your face, I am actually sad that this is happening. Take this as a lesson please, and do not go back to him. We know he isn't working and it kills us that you are responsible for everything when someone else is living there with you."

"Don't worry, Mom. I learned my lesson five times over. I'm fine… I feel better more than ever, more than I did since I have been with him," I laugh.

"He just had me worried. I should have known he was lying, like always. Did you go to work today?" she asks.

"No, I took today and tomorrow off. Helen said I had like eighty hours of PTO time, so I decided to use it, rather than let it expire, like always."

"You should use it. Tell Nolan I say hello and that I thank him for staying by your side through all of this, okay? You're lucky to have a friend like him. If you guys aren't busy tomorrow, stop down for dinner. Dad is making lasagna."

"I will. Okay, sounds good. I'll talk to you tomorrow."

I hang the phone up and sit down next to Nolan. "My mom says hi," I giggle and steal his cigarette.

"So I've heard."

"I can't imagine all of the untrue things that Tyler is telling people. I feel like I want to just lock myself in the house within the next upcoming week."

Nolan steals his cigarette back. "Listen, the people who really know you, they know that you aren't anything that he claims. It's fucking annoying, but don't let it bother you. Compared to all those low-lives, you actually are trying to live a normal existence. You work hard, pay your bills, mind your business or barely even go out. The people that he can easily convince don't even have jobs, or a home or aren't morally right with god either, so consider the sources," he reminds me.

I'm too tired to even speak. I lay my head on his chest, pull the blankets up and watch "Power" on the television. After he put his cigarette out, he throws the blankets over himself and puts his arm around me. If I had a remote I would freeze time right now. It's simple. It's quiet. It's relaxing. It's a break from the hell I constantly endure.

"Let's go out for lunch tomorrow. I have two more months of this partial unemployment, and all I have been doing is sitting in the house. I can't wait to be landscaping again," he says.

"I didn't know your job gives unemployment for the season… that's cool."

"If it's a nice day, we can work. Then, when we figure out our unemployment, we deduct the hours we worked in those two weeks and then the government pays the difference," he explains.

"Well, lunch sounds good tomorrow, considering you have like no food here for me to cook with."

"Oh shit, that's right, I can finally start eating good food every day now that you're staying here. How long do you think you're going to stay here? With this whole relationship thing, we have to figure something out. I don't want to rush into anything crazy, but I don't think it's a good idea for you to be alone at your apartment when Crazy finds out we're together."

Wow, I didn't think this conversation was going to happen so fast. I'm kind of caught off guard. "Honestly, I have no idea what to do. I don't have a lease for my apartment, since it's been up for like two years now. I don't care if I live there or here, but my apartment is fully-furnished and I don't want to get rid of anything. It won't all fit in here, since you have furniture, too," I point out.

He smiles at me. Not a normal smile, either; it's actually a happy smile. "I have a basement, Liza. Whatever we can't fit in my house you can store down there. I don't want you to get rid of anything. Plus, it doesn't hurt to have back-up furniture or appliances. Your stuff is nicer than mine anyway, so no argument here. I'll even put some of my shitty furniture down in the basement, if you want to use yours."

"Thank you," I say.

"For what?" he asks.

"I don't even know exactly, but thank you for always dealing with me and my drama from both the past and now. You giving us a try and being so laid-back about everything is a huge change for me."

He gives me a kiss. I turn the light off and we both fall asleep.

CHAPTER 13

"Wake up, lazy," Nolan says.

I turn around and pull the blankets up over my head. I'm the worst when it comes to waking up in the morning and that will never change, despite why or who I have to wake up for. In seconds, I feel the cold air hit my skin and that's it: I am pissed.

"Really?" I say, half asleep.

"If you want to pull the blankets over your head, I'll just pull the blankets off," he says.

I slowly sat up and take a drink out of the water bottle on the side of his bed. I pick my phone up and to no surprise I have texts from Tyler, as well as missed calls and voicemails. He makes me sick. I throw the phone down on the bed. "He won't stop texting or calling me," I say to Nolan.

He grabs my phone and scrolls through the various texts that this lunatic sent me. I didn't even care to read any of them.

"Do you want me text him from my phone? I won't be a dick, but I am going to tell him to cut it out with this constant bothering shit," he says.

"Just let it go. It will only make it worse on me. Plus, I still have to tell him that you and I are officially trying to make a relationship work. I'm sure once the word gets out, I am going to be labeled everything under the sun. They are going to say I was cheating on him and blah, blah, blah. He will never have to be accountable for the shit he has done to me," I say, getting aggravated.

Nolan gives me a weird look. "His feelings aren't worth sparing, since he never worried about yours. Too bad for him. He didn't appreciate you."

"I couldn't agree more. Actually, I'll text him after I wake up and get ready. Wait… don't you owe me lunch today?" I ask.

"Yes, I do. Get ready so we can go already."

I run into the bathroom, straighten my hair and throw some mascara and eyeliner on. I'm tired still, but I'm getting ready pretty fast. I run into his bedroom to grab my leggings, a t-shirt and a hoodie. As long as my hair looks cute, I can kind of bum it today.

"I'm going to warm the car up," he yells up the steps.

"I'll be down in two minutes, I'm just putting socks and shoes on. I'll meet you out there."

I put my shoes on, put my phone in my pocket, grab my purse and run down the steps. I make sure I looked decent, then meet Nolan in the car.

He turns the radio on, then asks, "Where do you want to go?"

"I haven't gone out to eat in a long time, so I don't care… you pick."

"Alright."

There goes my phone again, except its ringing this time. I pull it out of my pocket and see that it's Tyler.

"Just answer it, Aliza. See what he wants… not like it will be important, but you guys did just break up, so…"

I give Nolan a dirty look then answer the phone and put it on speaker. "What do you want, Tyler?"

"Did you really sleep over at Nolan's last night, scumbag?"

"You and I aren't together…why does it matter? Obviously you're only calling to argue like always," I say with an attitude.

"That's nice. You broke up with me a day ago and you're staying over some other dude's house. Everybody is going to see that I wasn't lying. I bet you were cheating on me the whole time we were together!" he yells into the phone.

I shouldn't have answered this because now I'm getting mad. "You lie about everything! I caught you cheating on me and left you. Besides that fact, you never come home and you still have no job. I am not doing this with you anymore. Who I talk to, where I stay and who I am with is none of your business. Stop fucking calling and texting me!"

"Or what, Aliza? Make me stop! Did it ever occur to you that I was talking to other women because my own girlfriend doesn't pay attention to me?" he spews out of his mouth.

I roll my eyes and look at Nolan, who I can see is getting angrier with every word Tyler says. I exhale smoke from my cigarette then go off. "Tyler, give the 'poor little me' act up! Nobody believes the shit you say because everyone knows exactly how you are! All you do is lie, steal and cheat. Your own friend's barely talk to you because of the things you do! I am done with you. I tried to make this work for years with no help from you! All I wanted from you was honesty and understanding. You flip out over everything and if you don't get your way, you turn into a lunatic! Not to mention, that you're a complete asshole! I am sick of living in an apartment with another person who doesn't hold their end of anything! I am so done!" I scream.

"God forbid you support your man when he is going through things. I should be able to rely on you for help," he says in a nasty tone.

"That's the thing – you want help with *everything*. You just don't want to find a damn job or act like a normal human being! That's your choice, which is exactly why I am moving out within the next two weeks. Keep the apartment, but all the bills and rent are yours to pay as of February 1st. Oh and everything in that place is mine, so I will be taking it," I scream back into the phone with every ounce of my voice.

"You know I can't afford that place without a job..."

All I can do is laugh, "Well, good luck. Hopefully you get a job or a sorry-ass girlfriend to pay for everything. In the meantime, stop calling me." And just like that, I hang up.

I look at Nolan and continue to laugh in an angry way. He just shakes his head in disbelief. Tyler is really that much of an asshole that he will try his hardest to do what he can to sabotage who I am. Nolan pulls into a parking spot at one of the local diners, which was a good choice on his behalf.

"I love their salads here!" I say excitedly, trying to get off of the subject of Tyler and me.

"You're excited over salads, seriously?" he mocks me.

I throw my cigarette butt and keep walking. "I don't get out much."

We walked into the restaurant, tell the hostess we need a "table for two, please" and follow her into the diner.

Once we are seated, she gives us our menus and leaves to get the silverware. It feels really good to be out for once, but I have this nervous feeling in the pit of my stomach. I feel like everybody and their brother will see Nolan and me, then go running back to Tyler. Although I am happy to be here and attempting public things with Nolan, I am worried about all the drama that is going to come with this. Shit will hit the fan full-force, and it hasn't even hit a little bit yet. Out of the corner of my eye, I see the waitress walking over to our table. I put the menu down and wait for her to arrive.

"Hello, my name is Kacie and I'll be your server today. Let's start off with some drinks..." she says with her pen and pad in hand.

"I'll take a Sprite." I look at Nolan and he nods his head,. "He'll have one, also," I say and smile.

"Are you guys ready to order or do you need a minute?"

"I could use a minute. Nolan?"

"Yes, I'll be ready soon," he says.

Kacie puts her pad and pen into her apron pocket and heads over to the fountain machine to get our drinks ready.

"Yo, you good?" he asks.

I peek over the top of my menu, "Yeah, just looking at the menu. I love their salads, but I'm so hungry that I don't know if that's what I want."

"I'm getting the bleu burger. It comes with a big order of fries. Get your salad and whatever else you want," he offers.

"Their salads are huge, so it would just be a waste to order something with it. I'm going to get their chef's salad and maybe I'll get an order of fries to bring home with us. Want to do that? I'll pay for them."

He puts his menu down and instantaneously our waitress is standing at the table with her pen and her pad ready. "Do you both know what you want to order?" she asks as she sets our drinks down and throws the straws on the table.

I look at Nolan to give him the go-ahead. He glances up and begins to order for himself. "I'll take the bleu burger with the side of fries. Can I have ranch on the side, please? And she'll take a chef's salad and we'll get an order of fries to go," he says.

We hand her our menus and she proceeds to the kitchen. This diner isn't too big, but the décor is really cool. Everything is very vintage; pictures of old cars, musicians, electric guitars, hues of reds, blues and blacks. It has a 1950's/1960's vibe and I love it.

"You good?" Nolan asks.

"Doesn't this place have the coolest décor? I love it. Every time I come here, I admire it, as if I've never seen it before," I say.

"I guess it's okay." He laughs and shrugs his shoulders.

"Guys are so clueless… you all can't appreciate the little things."

"Listen, I appreciate the little things like when they get my order right and all the food is hot. I don't pay much attention to anything else," he jokes.

We sit waiting for our food patiently, talking about nothing and enjoying our time. Then all of a sudden here comes one of Nolan and Tyler's mutual friends, Chris. I signal for Nolan to look to his left without making it noticeable, which he fails at.

Scooting off of his seat, he tells me he will be "right back". I just smile and nod my head. This is going to end great… NOT. Chris is a drama king too, maybe not as bad as Jason, but bad enough. Even though I am trying to keep my head down and out of sight, I can't help but keep looking over at Chris's table. He's with some girl who I've never met. No surprise there; he is a player.

Trying not to look interested, I decide to text Ally. I need some outside advice because this is going to end with a boom at some point today.

"Nolan brought me out for lunch… and guess who's here? CHRIS!!! All aboard the drama fest train later, 'cause you know it will be pulling up once he talks to Tyler."

I sent the text to Ally and thankfully I see Nolan coming back to our table. I know I probably look nervous as hell and that's because I am. I don't care if Tyler is hurt or upset. Face it – if he gave a shit about me, he wouldn't have done the things that he has done. However, I am nervous about him finding out that Nolan and I are attempting a relationship, especially this soon. I smile at Nolan as he scoots back into the booth.

"What did Chris have to say?" I ask, trying to appear nonchalant.

"Not much. He introduced me to his 'new girl', as he called her…she probably won't even make it to the weekend, but she is eating his attention up."

"Wow, I'm surprised he didn't mention anything about me sitting here…"

Nolan smiles. "Oh, he did. He asked if we were on a date, so I told him the truth. He seemed a little blown away by it. I think everyone is going to be in shock for a little bit. Hey, I don't really give a shit what Tyler has to say. I'm going to claim my girl, the girl he tried to destroy," he says, proudly.

"Oh, aren't you just the sweetest. You do know that this is going to be a little rocky for a month or two, right? Ty is going to start more than just an argument. This may turn into an all-out war because not only does he not have a job to pay for the apartment when I move out, but he also is going to have a bruised ego…I'm kind of dreading the next couple of weeks," I admit.

"He'll get over it, Aliza. He's the one who screwed up. You think I don't know him?

He can do whatever he feels is necessary because he isn't going to hurt you, harass you or anything else. I can handle his stupid ass. So chill and don't worry about it. I'll take care of whatever he throws our way."

I don't really know what to say. Luckily our waitress comes over just then, and so it's an easy conversation to drop. I honestly have lost my appetite now that I have myself worried, but I'm just going to ignore this feeling. My anxiety is so bad, especially when my intuition starts going into overdrive. While handing the salt to Nolan, I notice my phone vibrating against the table.

"You shouldn't worry about Tyler's drama. You needed to leave him, and I think Nolan made that possible. Without Nolan, you would still be with him… stop worrying about what drama he is going to start."

I read Ally's text and realize she is right, but walking away is easier said than done. I have to shake this shit off before it makes me sick to my stomach. I look up at Nolan and can't help but smile. I am very lucky to have this chance with him. Tyler isn't going to ruin it, but he is going to try like hell.

"How's that burger, slob?" I joke.

"Excellent. Are you sure you just want that salad? You are missing out on a damn good lunch."

"Yeah, I'm good. I'll enjoy those fries later, though."

For the next fifteen minutes we sit silently while stuffing our faces. This place has the best food!

"Yo, I'll hit you up later. See you later, Aliza," Chris says as he walks out of the diner.

"I bet he makes it a point to talk to Tyler today and narc on us," I say, rolling my eyes.

"So be it…I don't care, Liza. Like I told you a hundred times already, nobody is worried about Tyler," he says while waving the server over for our check.

"I know, I know," I say.

As fast as the waitress put our check on the table, Nolan snatches it up. He starts reaching for his wallet and I do the same. I'm not really sure if this is an official date – like do I pay or does he pay? Do we split the check? We can solve this dilemma by both paying. I start to put some cash on the table and he slides it back towards me.

"I got it covered. Put your money back in your wallet," he insists.

Before grabbing the money, I look up at him. "Are you sure? I brought money… we can split the bill."

He throws his money next to the bill then gets up. "Let's get out of here," he says.

I grab my wallet and slide out of the booth. While he is paying the waitress, I continue to his car. I am really happy that Nolan and I are dating… whoa, that is really weird to say. I just hope this doesn't crash and burn like Ty and me. Nolan opens his car door and gets in with a weird expression on his face.

"What's wrong?" I ask.

He just shakes his head and pulls out of the parking lot. Something is not okay. He looks pissed, extremely pissed off. I have no idea what could make him look this angry.

"Nolan, what's wrong? Two minutes ago you were fine and now you look like you are going to kill somebody. What's going on?" I ask worriedly.

"Listen, I don't want you to leave the house without me or someone else with you. Tyler just sent me this wild text saying that you need to 'watch your back' because he knows you were cheating on him with me all along," he says in a loud voice.

"That's bullshit! I never cheated on him. *He* cheated on me. There is no way to turn this on me. The sucky part is you and I are always together, so this is an easy lie for him to tell people, which will be believed. This is a goddamn joke," I yell, slapping my hand on the dashboard in frustration.

"You and I both know the truth, but I do think he is going to lose it when he sees you, be it night or day. I don't think he gives a shit who sees him go after you. I can't control you, but please don't leave without me or Ally or anyone else. If he gets ahold of you and hurts you, which he will try, I promise I will end up in jail. I'm not kidding!" he warns.

"I know. This isn't fair! I don't deserve to live in fear every damn day because of that psycho. Granted, him and I just broke up and now we are dating, but it has been over for a while now, both emotionally and physically. I don't care what anyone has to say – nothing a person says about me will ever be worse than the things he has said to me. This gets me so aggravated. People will fall for his shit and I will look like a scumbag," I say, shaking my head.

Nolan grabs my hand. "Screw him, okay? I will not let him lay a finger on you and as far as him running his mouth, consider the source." He gets out of the car, walks around the front and opens my door. "Just please have someone with you. If you have to go to your mom's or anywhere by yourself, take my car," he offers.

"Wow, you're going to trust me with your beautiful new baby?" I joke.

"Don't push it."

He shuts the front door behind us. Nolan can be an asshole, but he can also be a gentleman. Luckily I never had him act out of character towards me, but we have never really dated. I kick my shoes off and stash my container of fries in the refrigerator. Of course, I forgot to ask him if we can go grocery shopping or to my house. There is hardly anything to eat. Forget about condiments, there is nothing in there! I close the refrigerator and head upstairs so I can rip a piece of paper out of my journal. I need to write a list, regardless of if we go to my house or the store. I grab my journal and a pen and start to list what we need while he is in the bathroom.

"What's that?" he asks, pointing at my journal.

"A notebook... You have like no food or anything to cook with. I'm making a list of things that we need from my house and the grocery store."

"Do you think it's a good idea to go to your apartment?" he asks.

"Not really, but I'm going to text Alora real quick and see if she can stop by and knock on my door when she is coming home from work. I highly doubt he's there anyways, but I will double-check. I cannot deal with any unnecessary fighting if he is there."

He sits down beside me. "I'm not trying to be controlling, but you aren't going there unless someone is with you, and even that doesn't make me feel better. So whenever you have to stop there, I am going, too." He scoops me up and puts me on his lap. "Oh and another thing, I heard you tell Tyler that you are moving out. Are you moving into this place?" he asks, motioning to his room.

"Well, obviously. Where else am I going to go?" I ask, rhetorically.

"Cool. I'm happy that we are taking this really slow." He gives me a kiss and starts laughing.

I shoot him a dirty look, in a joking way. I finish my list then text Alora.

"Hey. Long story short, I left Tyler and I'm dating Nolan. Is there any way you can just run into my apartment and knock on my

door to see if Tyler is there? I need to get food because Nolan barely has anything here that is edible. I'll call ya later when I get everything settled. Don't say anything to Mom or Dad yet. I'm going to call Mom later."

I send the text message and rip my grocery list out of my journal. After I put the journal into my duffel bag, I go downstairs to get a drink. Nolan is in the front room on the phone with somebody. I feel my phone go off, which means Alora texted me back. I read the text to myself and then reply with a simple but heartfelt "thank you".

"Yep. I'll let ya know. You are lucky you texted me when you did, or I would have said nope."

"Good news, my sister is going to stop at my apartment and knock on the door. If he isn't there, we can go clean the refrigerator and cabinets out. I want to grab some clothes and shoes, too. I have to go in to the office tomorrow and all my work clothes are at my place," I inform him.

"Whatever you want. I have boxes down in the basement. I'll grab those now. Get some contractor bags out of the laundry room, too," he says.

"Whatever you say," I reply while giving him a salute.

Finally, my sister texts me back about twenty minutes later and tells me the coast is clear. Nolan and I get our shoes and coats on, grab the boxes and bags, and then proceeded to his car. He turns his stereo up and neither of us has much to say. I think he senses my nervousness, which I know he understands. Going over to my apartment to start getting my stuff out and clearing the food out can be a little risky. We have no idea where Tyler is, or if he is going to show up while we are there. Halfway through our ride, Nolan grabs my hand and holds it until we pulled up to my place.

CHAPTER 14

I grab the mail out of the mailbox, pick out what is mine and pass it over to Nolan. "Will you throw this in your car before we go upstairs? I don't want to leave it behind while we grab everything else."

He runs to the car, tosses the mail in and walks behind me as we go to my door. I unlock it and dread even going in. It's funny how this was once my home for years, but all of a sudden, I can't stomach to even be here.

"What the hell did he do to my place?!" I yell.

The living room is trashed. The coffee table is snapped in half, decorative pictures are smashed in their frames, and the whole thing is a mess. I don't even want to see the rest of this hellhole. I really want to turn around and leave, but I can't. I continue into the kitchen, the sink full of dirty dishes and the garbage overflowing. At this point I am beyond pissed, so I start throwing everything food-related into boxes. Cans, condiments, meats, dry food – you name it, I throw it in.

"Liza, go get your clothes and shit together – I'll take care of everything in here. If you want to get out of here quicker, we are better off splitting up," he orders.

"Good idea. I do just want to get out of here. This is ridiculous and uncalled for!"

During my walk through the living room, I kick the broken coffee table out of my way and let out a scream of anger. I shouldn't be surprised, but I am. The bedroom isn't as bad, thank God. He must have stayed out of here and slept on the couch. Without even thinking, I just start throwing everything from my closet into bags. I get that cleared out, tie the bag and toss it near the door. I begin to open my drawers and pile all of those clothes, socks and underwear into garbage bags, tie them and toss them by the door, too. I can't grab everything tonight, but I'm afraid to leave anything of value or that I like because he might destroy what's left when he notices the food and my clothes cleared out. I started to grab random trinkets – books and other things. I throw them all under the bed. I know he won't look there, since he has no reason to and is often blinded in his fits of rage. I begin to stuff everything I can fit under the bed, but then my hand brushes over a cold metal object. I quickly feel around to find it again, so that I can pull it out and have a look.

"Oh my God!" I scream.

Nolan comes running in. "What's wrong?" he asks, nervously.

My voice won't work. All I can do is stare at Nolan with my eyes big and my hand over my mouth. I start to get up, so I can show him what I found, but I can't move. The most I am able to do is hold the gun in the air for Nolan to see.

"HOLY FUCK! Aliza, put that down carefully and let me check it out. It could be loaded!" he instructs.

I gently lay the gun on the bed and walked away, still speechless. Nolan walks over to the gun, picks it up and begins checking it out. Sure enough, Tyler has left it loaded.

"Grab what you can lift and let's get these bags and boxes into the car," he says while taking the clip out of the gun and pulling something back to release the remaining bullet from the chamber. He then throws the bullets into one pocket and the gun into another.

Finally, the shock has resided. "But wait – I started to hide things under the bed, so he wouldn't ruin what I wasn't able to get. I figured he wouldn't look there because he would assume I took it all. You have to help me get that shit and put it under the couches and behind my armoire, please," I beg.

"Just start getting what you can and get it into the car. Grab what's under the bed and start loading it in. I'll follow you down with all the bags, since they're heavy, anyways. I need to get you the hell out of here," he demands.

I do as he says, and quickly. I grab everything that my hands can hold, since the items are loose. I make four trips from my apartment into the car and back again, in order to get everything. Nolan gets all of the bags in the trunk, along with my toaster, microwave and some other random things in the backseat. He lifts one of the two televisions and manages to fit it into his trunk, wrapped in every blanket, sheet and coat we can find, also cushioned with all of my bed pillows. The TV is rather big, so he has to bungee cord the trunk closed, as securely as he can.

"Aliza, you never knew he had this gun?" he asks.

I shake my head. "No, never in my life. The second my hand touched it, I knew what it was. I swear I could have thrown up when I saw it with my own eyes. I have no idea how long he had it under there," I explain.

"This is insane. He's too unstable to have this. You could have been friggin' killed!" he yells at no one in particular.

"Tell me about it," I say sarcastically. Then it hits me. "Wait, how do we know it's a gun registered to him or not? Is there a way we can find out who this gun is registered to?" I ask, knowing nothing about firearms.

"Here's the thing. I'm not too into this gun shit, so I might be wrong, but I think we would have to contact the police to run it. When you register a gun, it is registered with this number," he says while laying his finger on a long number on its side, so I can see it. "Each gun has its own serial number...all of the owner's information gets pulled up when they enter the number," he replies.

He throws the gun into his center console and pulls away from my apartment. I can't wait to just get the hell home and get this gun out of the car. Even though Nolan emptied the chamber, I still feel very uneasy with it being so close. I have no idea if this is a stolen gun or if Tyler bought it! With our luck, if we get pulled over and it was Ty's, he would probably say we stole it or something. He is acting like a psycho about Nolan and I dating, which means he will do anything in his power to cause problems for us.

"What kind of gun is that?" I question Nolan.

"It's a 9 millimeter, I think. When we get your shit in the house and at least halfway unpacked, I'll figure that out."

"You don't have to help me unpack. If you just help me carry everything into your room, I'll be happy to do that," I reply.

For the remainder of the ride, we listen to what is on the radio. He actually lets me put my station on, too. Like most of my friends, he listens to nothing but rap. Don't get me wrong; I like rap, but I can't listen to it all day. I need my alternative rock right now, and he knows that. I still can't believe I found that… *thing* in my apartment. What bothers me the most is the fact that I have no clue how long it has been under my bed. Tyler could have killed me in a split second. I could have been shot during one of his fits of rage or he might have shot me when I was sleeping. The scariest part about this is my life always was in his control, if you really think about it. This gun could have been under my bed for two years, two months, two weeks, two days, two hours… I have no idea!

Nolan pulls into his parking spot directly in front of his walkway, which works out great in tonight's case. We have a ton of bags, boxes and loose items to bring into the house. I'm so mentally exhausted right now!

There is no way in hell that I am putting everything away tonight, especially since I have to wake up early for work in the morning.

Nolan walks around the car. "Let me get this TV into the house first, then I'll help you grab the rest of the shit," he says.

"Wait… grab me like two or three garbage bags, so I can throw all this stuff into them. It will make my life a lot easier," I say while opening the front door for him.

"You got it, he winked."

He quickly places the television in the living room and comes out with the requested garbage bags. I start to throw everything from the backseat into a garbage bag, while he walks in and out of the house with boxes of food. I fill two and a half garbage bags with pictures, knick-knacks, books, décor, stuffed animals, and everything else under the sun. He probably thinks I am crazy for worrying about these things, but they are have a weird sentimental value to me. I bring the last two and a half bags into the bedroom. Surprisingly, Nolan is like the Flash and has every box and bag in the house before I could even blink. If anything, I have to at least get that food put away, so it doesn't spoil. Plus, after I put it all away, I'll know exactly what I need to buy. I kick my shoes off at the bottom of the steps, take my bra off and put it on the back of the couch. I am so exhausted!

"Here, smoke half of this," Nolan says, handing me his cigarette.

"No problem, bud. Want to help me put some of this away? I'm going to put all my clothes and stuff away after work tomorrow. Can you live with bags all over the bedroom for a night?" I joke.

"I'll live with bags all over my bedroom for a month, if that makes you happy."

I start laughing, "Well that's good, because that may be exactly what I do. Just get everything out of the boxes for me and I'll organize the refrigerator and cabinets." I take charge.

After he empties out the boxes, he gives me a kiss and goes to go take a shower. I'm just about done, when my phone rings… it's my sister.

"What's up?"

"Nothing. Are you going to tell me what happened with you and Tyler, or are you going to wait a few months?" Alora asks sarcastically. The attitude runs in the family.

"There's not much to say. I noticed his phone on the kitchen counter when he was sleeping, and obviously I went through it. Considering he learned this new trick called, 'I don't go home to my girlfriend five out of seven nights a week' very often, I think I had justification to do what I did."

"I mean you did, but what did you find?"

I laughed. "HA! What *didn't* I find?! I found dirty texts to and from some Maria. Then I found pictures of her boobs, times to meet up and just stupid conversations. All of that was enough!"

"So now you're dating Nolan? All of Middtown knows about you two, probably Mom and Dad, too… news travels quickly around here, as you know," Alora says.

"Do you think it's a bad idea to move on as fast as I did?"

"As far as anyone is concerned, you and Ty didn't exactly have a normal relationship. I think everyone felt relieved that you finally left him. Mom and Dad probably really do know by the way, that wasn't a joke. Want me to tell them at least, before you talk to them?"

I thought for a minute. "Actually, yes you can. Can you tell Mom that I was going to call her, but I told you I was tired and asked if you can let them know? Tell her I'll stop over tomorrow after work sometime. I promise."

"I'm going to jump in the shower, but sure. I have work and school tomorrow, but text me then," she says.

"Yep, I have work too. I'm literally going to do the same. See ya later," I say before hanging up.

All of the food is put away. I grab my bra and walk upstairs. I take sweatpants, underwear and a t-shirt out of a garbage bag, throw my phone on the bed, and then walk into the bathroom. Nolan is still in there. I hope he doesn't mind any company. I quietly undress, then hop in behind him.

"Oh hey," I say.

"I'm almost done, so you can have the whole shower to yourself. Of course, you need to wash my back in order to have the shower alone… that's the only stipulation," he says, while handing me the damp washcloth.

I grab his body wash and begin to lather the washcloth. I take my time washing every inch of his back, then hand him the cloth and my body wash. "Your turn," I smile.

He takes the cloth and pours my body wash on the rag while I turned around. I haven't had this experience, ever. I know it sounds stupid to be happy over something like this, since it's just something little and stupid.

Who would have known that a simple back scrub could make a person this happy?

"You good?" he asks.

"Yes, I am. Thank you."

"I'm going to get a drink then lay down. You coming to bed when you're done?"

"Oh my god, yes I'm so tired. I can't wait to lay down with my pillows and pass out. I'll be out in five minutes."

Once he shuts the door, I get out of the shower and dry off quickly. I cannot get into his bed fast enough… my bed… *our* bed! Tomorrow is my first day back to work after my long weekend, so I need an adequate amount of sleep. I don't have to wake up at my normal time, since Nolan is going to drop me off. I brush my teeth, throw on an old t-shirt and shut the light off behind me

CHAPTER 15

"Liza, wake up…your alarm has been going off for like an hour," I hear Nolan, faintly.

All I can do is wave him off and turn around. I hate waking up! He has to get used to me setting one hundred alarms because this is my life. I pull the blankets over my head and silence the alarm for another ten minutes. He lays beside me and scoops me up. Another ten minutes goes by and I know I have to get up, but he is so warm and I hate the cold.

I throw the blankets off and sit up. "I'm going to brush my teeth and get dressed. Do you need a drink or anything?" I ask him.

"Nah, I'm good. Unlike you, I don't mind waking up for the day," he says, laughing.

"Why are *you* waking up at seven o'clock?"

"Well, did you forget that you aren't walking today?" he replies.

"Oh shit, that's right. I have to get used to not walking. I am hoping now that I can save up money and get myself a car," I smile.

"You will be getting a car… don't worry. I won't make you pay all the bills yet," he jokes. "I was thinking, if you want I can call Shawn and see if he can get his Uncle Dean's truck, and we can move some of your furniture out of your old place. I'll have someone find out if that asshole is there before I go, though, so don't worry."

"That sounds good. I want it out of there ASAP. The more time everything is there, the more opportunity he has to destroy it all." I walk into the bathroom.

I throw warm water on my face, dry it and then plug my hair straightener in. God, it had been a long weekend, and I am not ready to be an adult today. I don't even feel like putting make-up on today. I have to wear mascara and eyeliner no matter what, though. I'm sure I can do without it, but I've worn it every day since sixth grade. At this point, I put it on without even realizing it. I run the straightener through my hair a few times, pull it into a half-pony and finish getting dressed. I throw on black leggings with a black and white Ralph Lauren sweaterdress, UGGs and even throw a black headband in. Just another day at the office…

"You almost ready? Let's stop at Dunkin', so you can grab a tea or something…" Nolan says, knocking on the door.

I open the door and throw my pajamas in a pile of dirty clothes in the hallway, "I'm ready. Make sure you grab the hamper at my apartment," I say.

"You got it," he throws me the keys. "Start the car, I'll be out in a minute," he says.

I catch the keys, then walk into the bedroom to get my charger, journal and my purse. Shit, I need to grab something for lunch. I totally forgot about that, so I'm going to toss some snacks into my purse, too. I walk downstairs, get the snacks, put my coat on and then walk to the car. I wonder if Nolan will let me take this out without him, ever. Nolan treats this thing like a goddamned baby. Today better not drag by, since I haven't been at work in a few days. He gets in the car and grabs my hand while he is waiting to pull out. I have to admit, this is pretty nice. I'm not used to actually having another person act like they're into me, especially in public.

"Welcome to Dunkin'. What can I get you?" the voice rings out over the drive-thru speaker.

"Can I have a large coffee, black with 10 sugars..." He turns towards me.

"I'll get a tea with lemon and 8 sugars," I say while trying to gather dollars out of my purse.

We get to the window, he hands me my tea and refuses to take my cash. This whole being-paid-for thing is something I most definitely am not used to. Tyler never paid for a damn thing for me or himself, actually.

"I have money," he says.

"Yeah, I know, but I'm not used to being treated. I usually pay for everything."

"Well, not anymore."

He pulls right in front of the door and before I can gather my things, he leans me over and gives me a kiss. The weirdest part is that all of the office employees looking outside can see that I am not with Tyler. I'll explain it when they ask, but until then my lips are sealed. The biggest lesson I will gladly teach anyone is to never mix your personal life with your work life. I succeed more than not when it comes to leaving my personal life at the door; it rarely comes into work with me because I would never do my job the right way if it did.

"Listen, I'll be here a few minutes early, parked and waiting for you, but just in case, stay inside until I text you. Shawn already found out that Tyler isn't at your apartment. He is being really quiet, so you and I know that he has something brewing. I don't need him waiting outside your job, ready to pounce," he warns.

"I got it, bud, don't worry," I say with a thumbs up.

He shakes his head and gives me a playful shove out of the car. I turn around and poke my fingers into his side to tickle him. I shut the door and blow him a kiss. He flips me off and laughs while he slowly pulls away until I am inside of the building. It has been a long time since I came to work in a good mood. I clock in, take off my coat and sit down at my desk. There are so many doctor's orders on this desk and a million sticky notes. I wonder who covered for me.

"Well hello, Miss Aliza. Long time no see," Helen greets me.

"Hey, Helen. How have the last couple of days been without me?"

"Oh you know, a disaster. We are happy you're back. I hate to say it, but you have a stack of doctor's orders to mail out and although that part-timer Rebecca is a very nice girl, she doesn't have a clue about anything," she replies.

"I know, I said that in the past, too. In her defense though, she does work weekends and all she has to do is answer the phone and maybe show a family member or performer where they have to go for activities."

Helen slowly walks behind the desk and leans down. "We have a real serious meeting today at noon. There was an incident here over the weekend with a resident and an aide, and the family is livid. Apparently, this resident had an item go missing and her roommate witnessed this specific aide take it. I don't know specifics; I guess we will all find out what resident, what the item was and who the aide is later," she whispers.

"Can I take another day off? It's still early enough that nobody knows that I'm here yet. I can probably sneak out very easily," I joke.

She just laughs and walks into her office. I sorted the doctor's orders into piles according to each doctor's name. I grab some envelopes and address stickers and begin to file and label the envelopes. The phone hasn't start ringing yet, so I am able to get those orders sorted out and into the outgoing mail tray in no time. It is pretty calm at work this morning, so far. I pull my phone out of my purse to sneak a look at my messages. I'm in the habit of turning my phone ringer and vibrate setting off when I'm at work because the front room is so quiet. I feel like the other office workers can hear it when they have their doors open. Surprisingly, I already have one incoming text from Nolan.

"Hey, I just got to your apartment. We have the truck for about 3 hours. We will try to get everything out before he gets back. Did you contact your landlord yet, since the tenant downstairs keeps peeking out his window?"

Of course Ben is peeking out his window. He can never mind his own business. It's like he swears he is the property manager or something. I have lived there longer than him; he hasn't even been there for three years. I open the message up and begin to reply.

"Awesome! You guys are the best! I'll send Jen a text right now. Thank God for not

renewing the lease after it was up. Please try to take everything. NOTHING is his, furniture-wise. If you need to call me or something, call my work. My phone is on silent and it's going in my purse after I text my landlord."

Just in the nick of time, I throw my phone in my purse and look up to see the administer, Kristianne Simon, standing over my desk. I pull out a lip balm and play it off like that was my purpose for going in my purse.

I put the cap on my chapstick and put it in my pocket. "Good morning! Can I help you with anything?" I ask in a chipper tone.

"Yes, actually." She hands me a paper, "See the numbers on this left side? Can you please call them and let them know that their family member was in contact with another resident who has active shingles? Just let them know the procedure and everything that I have written on this paper. Make sure you tell them to call Diane Masey, our Director of Nursing, if they have any questions or concerns. Let them know that Diane will be in meetings until three o'clock, which is why *you* are calling. Surely, they will understand when you explain to them that you are calling by request of Diane, and Amber the Assistant Director of Nursing, considering their meetings and the urgency of this issue," Kristianne explains.

I grab the paper and stick it next to my notebook. "Do you need this copy back, or can I cross out the names and numbers that I had success with?"

"That's your copy, I don't care what you do with it," she says.

"Alrighty, I'm on it," I reply.

"Thank you! You are a life-saver. All department heads will be in a meeting soon and God only knows how long it will carry on for. After that we have to go over the tags from state. Luckily, there wasn't anything serious, but that's protocol."

When she turns around to walk away, I grab my highlighter and pen, this way I can highlight the successful calls. This is going to take at least an hour and that isn't counting the conversations that might drag on with a resident's family member. I didn't bring much for lunch today, just those few snacks. I guess that works out well because I can remain at my desk, rather than go into the break room to eat.

"Wait – I'll find someone to answer the phones, so you can get through that list," she says while walking out the doors.

I smile at her comment, then get right to work. After almost two hours and several unhappy families, I get through the list with only a handful of families who didn't answer. I'm surprised that some families don't have answering machines, which means I have to call them back until somebody picks up. Luckily, this project can be finished tomorrow. I can't wait to get home. I am dying to see what Nolan was able to salvage from my apartment.

"Shit! I forgot to text my landlord," I say to myself. I pull my phone out of my purse and begin texting her. All of the department heads are still in a meeting and will probably be in there until I clock out. It's pretty nice that I don't have to hide my phone.

"Hello, Jennifer. How are you? I hate that I have to text you on these terms, but Tyler and I broke up and it is in my best interest that I move out of the apartment. I am really upset, considering it has been my home for so many years now. January will be paid for in full, on time, like always. I will have the house spotless when I get everything out of there. I know this is kind of short notice, but it was a rather fast decision that I had to make in order to protect myself from Tyler. Not only has he cheated on me, but he has become pretty abusive, so I have no choice.

Again, I am extremely saddened by this awfully fast choice that I had to make for many reasons – the main one being I love that apartment. It was my first apartment and I am so happy that you allowed me to live there. Thank you for everything."

I send the text and put my phone on the desk. For some reason, my eyes start to water and I am hit with a quick shot of pain in my throat from trying to hold back the tears. Oh god! I am at work, I cannot cry. I quickly stand up and walk over to the window, in order to quickly focus on something and distract myself. To say that I'm not a fan of change is an understatement. I don't like change; therefore, I try to avoid it as often as possible and I have always been successful with that tactic. However, in the nineteen years of my life, I have never had so much change in such a short amount of time. My whole life is shifting and I know it's for the better, but I'm starting to feel very overwhelmed. Once I am able to calm down, I go back to my desk and within a few minutes, my landlord replies.

"Aliza, honey – I am so sorry to hear that your relationship ended that way. You never renewed a lease. As a result, you have the right to move out whenever you want. I am

so sad that you will be leaving the apartment, but I am very happy that you are putting your safety and happiness first. Is Tyler moving out, too?"

I quickly begin to type a reply, thankfully without the theatrics and dramatics that I have been so prone to lately.

"Thank you, Jennifer. I really do feel terrible about leaving, but I need to start fresh and I think moving will be the final message to Tyler that I am done. Honestly, I have no idea about his plans. He has no job; I have been the one upholding all the financial responsibility for a while now. He is going to have to find a job sooner or later

because I am gone. Your best bet is to contact him and see what his plans are. At this point in time, I try to remain no-contact with him, due to his demeanor regarding this break-up. He turned into a very violent person and it doesn't take much to set him off."

Although I see she is responding, I throw my phone into my purse and try to contact the families who I was unable to reach earlier. I only have a little while left until work is over; I might as well attempt to stay occupied. I have no idea who is answering the phones. Kristianne didn't really specify who she was putting in charge of that. I hear my phone vibrate against everything in my purse within seconds of putting it in there. I really need this conversation to end… at least just until I clock out.

"As far as I am concerned, if you aren't going to live there, neither is he. You are a wonderful girl! It breaks my heart that he has treated you so poorly. I don't want to rent to a person like that. Keep in mind, you have kept that apartment in pristine condition, so I owe you your security deposit of $600.00. I will give that to you in the form of a check on the first of February. Also, you don't owe me for January because when you signed the lease, you paid your first and last

month's rent, along with the security. If you need references for any future apartments or anything at all, please list my name and number. Keep in touch, and be well."

That's right – I don't owe her for January! In addition to not having to pay the six hundred dollars, I get my security back, too! I am so happy that I can deposit this money into my account. That's an easy twelve hundred dollars that I can put away for the future. For my new life.

"Thank you so much. I appreciate it more than you know! I am actually moving in with a friend for the time being. I'm upset that I have to move out in the first place, so the

last thing I want to do is look for a new place in a rush. Don't worry, I will keep you updated along the way."

It is so quiet in the front of this building. Everyone is in a meeting and whoever is answering the phone is picking it up on the first ring. They're pretty good, I have to admit. I should probably let Tyler know that the apartment is no longer mine as of February first, and nor is it his. I hope he can work something out for himself. Throughout this time with him, I wish I could be careless when it comes to his well-being. Apparently, I can't find it in my character to be as hurtful as he was. I haven't updated my disastrous life on paper for a couple days, and it's overdue. It feels good to open this journal, and I have no idea why or how this notebook gives me the amount of comfort that it does. But it's almost like having a friend within myself, and that makes me feel better.

Entry #79

Beside Nolan and I dating, I'm moving out of my apartment. My life is either very boring and calm or completely ridiculous and overwhelming. Although all of these changes are positive things, so much is going on at one time and it is making my head spin. I haven't talked to Tyler since the day Nolan took me out for lunch. I hope Nolan was able to remove everything because whatever is left there, Tyler will trash. He might even trash the apartment itself, now. SHIT! I need Nolan to get those locks changed immediately.

Always,

Change, Changes

I quickly pick up my work phone and dial Nolan's phone number. I think Shawn is helping him, so I'm hoping Nolan can have him run and get new locks! It has to be done *now*. Once it is taken care of, I will let Jen know and explain why I had to do it. She won't care; if anything, she should be grateful. Morally, I would feel like shit if he trashed her place. Plus, I want my damn security deposit back! After several rings, Nolan answers.

"Babe?"

"Well, that's a first…what's up?" he asks.

Stuttering because of how fast I am trying to speak, "C-can you please have Shawn or whoever is helping you go get new locks as soon as possible? Regardless of whether we get all my stuff out, Tyler is going to snap and trash the apartment."

"Did you talk to your landlord yet? Are you even allowed to do that?"

"Yes, I spoke to her about moving, but she doesn't know that I'm changing the locks. Don't worry, she will appreciate it. I'll let her know as soon as it is done. I'll make her a key over the weekend and I'll drop it off to her," I say.

"Okay. I'll have Shawn go now because we were just finishing up the last load. The apartment is empty. We just have to straighten it up, vacuum… do little shit like that," Nolan informs me.

In my business-like tone, I reply, "Thank you. It is always appreciated. Have a nice day!"

"Your work voice is way nicer than your normal voice," he says, laughing before I hang up.

I hang the phone up as Helen is walking into her office. She does not look happy! I'm not sure if I should ask what happened, or wait until she approaches me.

CHAPTER 16

After answering a couple of calls, it is time to go and it's odd that Helen hasn't come out of her office. I can't imagine what has this upset. She told me the meeting was requested by family, due to something being stolen and really nothing more. Now that I think about it, the meeting did run rather long. I straighten up my desk, leave a little note to remind myself to have the stockroom staff Cher order more stamps and envelopes when I come in tomorrow, put my coat on, grab my purse and clock out. However, Nolan isn't here yet. It isn't exactly 4:00 P.M., so I'll just sit in the lobby. I was going to go out front, but decide to try and start a conversation with Helen.

"Hey Helen, I'm clocked out. I'll be leaving as soon as my ride gets here, hopefully within the next few minutes." I give her my daily departing heads-up.

"Have a good night, Aliza. I'll see you tomorrow," she replies.

I stand there for about thirty seconds before I feel my phone vibrating. It's Nolan calling.

"Hey, I'm outside," he says.

I hang up the phone without saying a word. I am dying to know what happened in that meeting. I throw my phone in my purse and hurry out the doors and into his car. Once I sit down and shut the door, I am greeted with a kiss.

"How did the whole lock-changing thing go?' I ask, pulling away from his lips.

He hands me the new key. "Good. I can get a few copies of this key made tomorrow when you're at work. I figured I would finish what needs to be done in your place anyway. I won't have anything to do tomorrow."

"If you want to straighten it up, that's fine. I do want to stop there tomorrow after work or even over the weekend. I want to make sure everything is up to par. I also want to take pictures, in case that scumbag gets in. Even though the locks are changed, we have to make sure all of the windows are locked, too," I tell him.

"We already checked them, so don't worry," he reassures me.

"I have to let him know about this, which is why I wanted to make sure everything was locked up. He is going to flip, and I don't want that place in shambles."

He proceeds to drive without saying much to me. It seems like he has been in a weird mood since I told him I had to talk to Tyler about the apartment going up for rent. I don't think he is mad or anything, but he seems a little annoyed. I light a cigarette and I swear, the first smoke after my shift is always the best! I would love to smoke the whole thing, but I'm going to give Nolan half so I can use it to open up a conversation, as always.

"Here, babe," I say, as I hand him the cigarette.

He takes it and smiles, "Thanks."

"Not that I think you care, but are you cool with me calling Tyler about the apartment?" I ask.

He grabs my hand "It's cool... I just hate his attitude towards you and how goddamn disrespectful he is. I get it, though – this is something that you need to tell him, especially because he doesn't need to go there and fuck the place up," he replies.

We pull up to his house... our house, whatever. Nolan gets out of the car, opens my door and takes my purse. I guess chivalry isn't dead yet. I always knew Nolan was a good guy, but being able to have him in my life on this level makes me realize exactly how fast I am falling for him. I pray this doesn't ever end and believe me, I don't pray much.

He puts my purse on the counter, then gives me a hug. "Shawn called and asked if I can help him with his car. I guess something is going on with the fuses and he has no idea how to fix it. Do you care if I run over there?" he asks.

"Of course not," I say, laughing.

"What are you laughing at?"

"It's so funny to go from that asshole just leaving and then you asking to leave, communicating with me. It's a nice change, though," I say.

He walks over to the fridge and pulls out a blue Gatorade. "Well, you can come if you want, or I was going to leave my car because I know you said you want to check the apartment out and run to the store."

I grab the Gatorade off of him and am caught off guard when he said he would leave his car for me to use. Without saying a word, I jump on top of the counter and pull him over. This all seems so stupid, to be this happy over him just being a normal boyfriend and offering his car or asking if he can go out, but to me it is such a huge deal. I can't help myself; I grab him and start kissing him. My heart will never be the same, but it will get better with time.

"You have fun with Shawn," I joke, "and I'll run over and make sure everything is okay at my place. I'm going to bring a few things to wipe the walls, windows and appliances down. The quicker I get that place emptied and clean, the quicker it will all be behind me. I do need to do some grocery shopping too, because you bachelors have no clue how to eat like adults."

"Okay, sounds good. Shawn knows that I planned on leaving the car for you, so he is picking me up in the death trap. Oh, I'll have so much fun. Maybe I'll even eat some more junk food, too," he exclaims sarcastically.

He walks upstairs to get changed – no need to ruin the outfit he has on, I'm assuming. In the meantime, I think it might be a good idea to have someone come to the apartment with me. I haven't talked to Tyler, so I have no idea if he knows I moved everything out. I have a feeling he hasn't been there because if he had been, he would have been texting me about his gun… at least, I think he would. I pull my phone out of my purse and text my sister.

"Hey, I have to run to my apartment and clean it up a bit. Are you busy?"

I'm hoping someone can accompany me. I'll just copy-and-paste that text to Alora, and also send it to Ally and hope one of them answer. I hate getting so nervous. It isn't that I'm afraid of Ty, I just don't want to deal with him. Okay, maybe I am afraid of him, but I have good reasons for that.

A person like him will take everything from a person, physically, mentally and emotionally. A narcissist will drain everything you possibly have. They feed off of your energy, pride and self-confidence. The way gasoline propels a vehicle, a narcissist is fueled by our stolen self-confidence. They syphon it out with every negative word they say to you. Then, once their ego has enough gas, they leave you empty.

"Liza, Shawn just texted me – he's out front. Please be careful, and I'd rather you not go to the apartment by yourself, only because I don't want you to get hurt. If you can't get someone else to go with, screw it. We will take care of it another day," he says, walking into the living room.

"Believe me, we are on the same page about that finally," I say after I kiss him goodbye.

Once he shuts the door, I run upstairs, change my clothes and get into sweat pants and a hoodie. If I can't get ahold of anyone, I'll just run to the supermarket. Not to mention, Nolan left me his car! I think I might go for a joy ride, too. I can find enough adventures to keep myself busy until he is done helping Shawn. I feel my phone vibrate in my pocket and the second I see the texts from both Ally and Alora, I know the apartment cleaning was out of the question. All I want to do is get that place, and everything is that connected to Tyler, behind me. The quicker I can cut all ties with him, the quicker I can heal myself and stop having to worry. I open my phone and start to text Nolan.

"Hey, Ally and Alora can't come with me, so I won't be cleaning the apartment tonight. Is

there anything you want me to grab from the supermarket? Where are your keys at?"

I send the text and throw my phone back into my pocket. I walk into the bathroom and start to touch up my eyeliner and mascara. I kind of feel like wiping it all off, but whatever. I'm stressed out and that makes the littlest things seem like a lot of anxiety-inducing work. Nolan quickly texts back.

"The keys are in the silverware drawer and that's fine. Just make sure you grab some soda. If you need money, grab a couple of twenty dollar bills from my top dresser

drawer. There should be a couple hundred there… take what ya need."

I send a simple text and thanked him for the offer, but I would be fine without his money. I don't think it will kill me to go and *see* the apartment, at least. Tyler has to know it is cleared out, and I am sure he knows the locks are changed. I get my coat on, grab my purse and Nolan's keys, and start towards the door. I turn the lights off behind me, shut the door and locked it. Out of the corner of my eye, I can see someone standing on the left side of the house and then it hits me. Tyler. Before I can move, he is walking towards me.

"Where's your boyfriend?" he sneers sarcastically.

"He's in the house, let me go get him," I lie.

"You're a goddamn liar. I saw him leave. So you're alone now."

I quickly fish around my bag for the keys and before I can grasp them in the bottom of my purse, Tyler grabs me by the arm.

"Let me go, Tyler. Now." I try to stay calm.

"No. You are going to talk to me like an adult and admit that you have been lying about just being Nolan's 'friend.' We both know it's been more than that."

Trying to wiggle my arm out of his hand, he starts to squeeze tighter.

"What the hell? Let me go. I'm not doing this," I demand.

He smiles. "Neither am I. I warned you both not to mess around and you guys didn't want to listen. You try to be slick and blame me for our relationship ending. Now you are going to talk, and I'm not taking no for an answer," he says.

"I will call the police. I'm not kidding. I will not say a word to you. I have nothing to say. We are done. Broken up. The apartment is emptied out and you and I are over. I don't know how many ways I can say that," I start to jerk my body around, in order to loosen his grip.

"You scumbags changed the locks, too. I have nowhere to go. Give me the goddamn key to the apartment, and I want my gun back. You are going to open Nolan's door. We are going in together and you are giving me the new key and my gun," he yells.

"I'm not doing anything… I don't know what the hell you're talking about. We don't have a gun, and you shouldn't, either."

In one quick motion, he opens his hand and smacks me in the face. He misses my mouth, and immediately I feel the force of his hand and the sting from his hit. At this point, all I can do is attempt to get away, but where would I even go? I doubt I can get into the house or lock the door, and he's going to get in... he's too close. I could escape and run off the porch, but where the hell would I run to? He's faster than me.

I'm screwed, I cry to myself in defeat. I begin to panic and started to squirm around, kicking my feet and swinging my fists.

"LET ME GO!"

Begging is an action that can make a person feel demeaned, powerless, and frantic, but it can also be helpful sometimes. A person like him is fueled by the act of controlling another human being. Sometimes begging is the only thing that will convince a narcissist to show mercy, because it's an act of submission at their own hands. It's the best high they could feel... and that's what I do. I beg. I beg, I act submissive... But it doesn't work.

Before I know it, I am on the ground, while he looms over me, smiling the most screwed-up, slimiest, sadistic grin that I have ever seen. As I start to move back toward the bannister, all I can feel is the rubber part of his shoe collide with my face.

CHAPTER 17

"Aliza... Aliza Leigh... can you hear me?" says an unfamiliar voice.

I can hear this man! I just can't seem to open my eyes and focus on my surroundings. Why am I struggling like this? Why does it all seem so bright? Why do I feel this intense pain in my face? Why do I deserve to go through this?

"Why...?" That's all I can say.

"Take your time, we aren't in a rush. I see you trying to open your eyes, so just take it easy", the doctor reassures me, Physically reacting to my commands is all I need from you right now, Miss Leigh," says the stranger.

Finally, I slowly open my left eye and then my right eye, not too long after.

"I can barely see anything in my right eye! My right eye isn't opening. Why isn't my… why isn't my eye opening?"

Then it hits me. All the pain on the right side of my face, it hits me in full force. First, I feel it in my head, similar to a migraine, but a more of a lightning bolt kind of pain. This is followed by intense pain that is radiating through my jaw, restricting me from opening my mouth very much.

I have been hit, kicked and pushed, and suffered through every other physical action that falls in the abuse category. Yet, this feels different. This is worse. This is serious. This is dangerous. This is abuse in its purest form. This is the last time.

Staring at the ceiling, I realize that I am laying in a hospital bed! Not just any hospital bed – the hospital bed that I was laid in because I'm pretty sure my ex-boyfriend put his hands on me, again!

"What the hell am I doing here?" I ask nobody in particular.

"Liza, babe... I came home and you were unconscious, on the ground in the corner of my porch. Please tell me what happened while I was gone… please?" Nolan questions me in a gentle voice.

Hardly being able to open my mouth, let alone speak, I put my head down and try my best to piece together what happened.

"Listen, I… I don't know. I just wanted to go to the store. I walked out of the house and Tyler was across the street. Next thing I know…" I can't finish my sentence. The pain I feel is unbearable.

I take a few minutes to let the pain ease a bit.

"We got into an argument. He wouldn't leave. He wanted the keys and the…" I stop.

"What did he want, Aliza? This is serious, *What did he want?*"

I try to sit up, in order to scan the room, and that's when I realize that my purse isn't in here.

"Shit! Nolan, where is my purse?" I panic.

"I don't know, the house? Why? You didn't have it when I found you on my porch. Aliza, what the hell is going on?"

"Nolan, he wanted the keys to my apartment and the… thing we found under my bed. I didn't have my set of keys on me, but I had your set. You need to go home and see if he got in your house and took that gun," I whisper.

Instantly, Nolan's nostrils started to flare and then his wrists tighten into fists. He is ready to lose it. Did I do the wrong thing by telling him, or was it the right thing? My life is a disaster, and with every good thing that is happening, something bad follows.

Walking into the room is an older doctor. "Hello, Miss Leigh. I'm happy to see you awake and alert. Let me brief you on the circumstances that brought you here, although I'm sure your companion has briefed you on the story from the police," he says in a soft tone.

"Okay," I reply.

"By the way, I'm Dr. Mathewson. Mr. Jackson found you unconscious on his porch. Clearly, that resulted in you having been here for the last four hours. Now, due to the head trauma that you experienced, we want to observe you here to make sure nothing more was transpiring. You have no concussion, surprisingly. However, we do want you to stay for a few more hours, in order to run additional scans. We'd rather be safe than sorry.

"We did find a minor fracture in your right jawbone. At this moment in time, you do not need any surgical repair, but you will need a series of follow-up appointments with an orthopedic doctor of your choice. The goal is to have the jaw fracture heal on its own over time, and then surgery will be ruled out. If, in fact, it doesn't heal correctly, then surgery will be needed. I'm sure that won't need to be an option, though, with the proper care. I will give you a printout with names and numbers of Orthos, along with your discharge papers… when the time comes. It shouldn't take longer than two hours for the whole kit and caboodle to be done, read and diagnosed.

"Miss Aliza Leigh, you are very blessed to only have a jaw fracture. Besides the immense swelling around your eye and jaw, bruising on your cheek and bruising around your eye, I have no clue how you walked away with just a minor fracture… frankly, myself and the rest of my staff are flabbergasted by your strength! Anyway, I'll be here for the remainder of the night, if you have any questions or concerns. Now, due to the nature of the call, we did have to inform the police. I have to send them in to see you, and in the meantime I will give you and your boyfriend time alone," he finishes.

I look up and in a loud, raspy whisper, I say, "Thank you."

Once he shuts the door, I look at Nolan, who is already sending a text to somebody. I can't even imagine what how he feels, having to find me like that.

I ask Nolan, "What do I do?"

"With what, Liza?"

"Nolan, there are cops here. What do I do? I've never spoken to police before," I say in a panic.

He looks up at me and puts his phone in his pocket. "You know he isn't going to stop. As much as I don't mess with the cops, you should tell them the truth. If you don't, then Tyler is going to keep hurting you, and I promise you, right now… that shit is going to blow up. I'm not sitting idly while he's stalking my damn house and putting his hands on my girlfriend.

"Tell them what happened. In the meantime, Shawn's running to the house to see if Tyler took the gun. When we leave this hospital, I'm bringing you home, helping you get settled and then you need to call your mom or sister and have them come over, because I have to handle something with this scumbag," he says all in one breath.

"If that's what you think I should do, I guess I have no choice, since I'm already here."

I close my mouth to lessen the pain, which doesn't do much, but it does enough. I'll do anything to have even the smallest bit of relief from the throbbing.

"I just don't want to deal with the headache of court and cops and people holding this against me," I cry.

Nolan looks at me with an expression that I don't recognize. I wouldn't say it was a look of pity. Maybe it's more sorrow than anything. Whatever kind of look this is, the concern, the anger and a heaping spoonful of sadness that I see – it's overwhelming and is making me cry more.

I look down for a minute. I still can't believe that I'm in this position. As much as I hate admitting when people are right, Nolan is right. He is *extremely* right.

"Tell the officers to come in," I say, feeling defeated.

He gets up and starts walking towards the door, but as much as I need to do this, I also need Nolan's support.

"Can you stay in here, please?"

He nods his head and gives me a faint smile, while walking out to invite the officers in.

This is my life. How ridiculous this whole situation is, and how crazy it is that Tyler hurt me to the point of being unconscious and needing to come here. I shut my eyes, trying my hardest to take this all in. All the pain, regret, anger, stress – and now I have to speak to police. I hear the door open and the footsteps of Nolan and two officers. I think there might be two officers, or maybe it's just Nolan, an officer and the doctor. Regardless, I pick my head up, not wanting to open my eyes… well, my eye. I don't want to talk to them, although I have to. I want to keep my eyes shut forever, but I know they will still be there waiting for a statement. Opening my eye to see police feet from my face isn't a good feeling, even if you are on the innocent end of the story. I look to my left and Nolan is sitting there in silence, staring at me with that look again.

"Hello, Miss Leigh. I'm Officer Hilling, and this is Officer Michaels."

Hello Miss Leigh," Officer Michaels says.

"How are you feeling? We are here because it's hospital protocol to call the police in any case of abuse. Dr. Mathewson said that you are willing to talk to us about your recollection of the incident you were involved in," Officer Hilling states.

I look up at him and inhale deeply, letting the breath back out. "I...I was attacked by my ex-boyfriend. His name is Tyler Smith." That's all it took; the tears start pouring from my eyes, as I feel a burning sensation in my throat.

I watched as the officer scribbled my explanation onto a piece of paper. He is awfully tall and husky. The width of his shoulder span is impressive, especially with his muscular arms. Looking all the way up at his face is not an easy task, because the strain to do so makes my head hurt worse.

"All I did was walk out of Nolan's house. I was on my way to the supermarket. Before I knew it, Tyler came from the left side of the porch and grabbed me. I told him to leave me alone and all I remember is being thrown to the ground." I cry some more.

My voice barely audible, I look down and say, "I think he has a gun on him and I'm terrified," and that is my breaking point.

What starts out like normal crying turns into me having a full-on panic attack. The kind that makes you feel like your throat is closing into itself and something is on your chest causing it to feel tight and heavy. The tears come gushing out of my eyes like water breaking through a dam… fast and uncontrollable, as I start shaking. I need to get a grip!

I can barely get air into my lungs and at this point, I'm crying so hard that I can't make a sound. The sobbing is causing nearly debilitating pain in my face, but it doesn't stop me. Everyone in the room just stands there and looks around awkwardly. After what seems like an eternity, I finally pull myself together…kind of.

Officer Hilling takes a small notepad out of his breast pocket and grabs a pen out of the notebook binding. "What causes you to believe he has a gun? Did he pull the weapon out on you, Miss Leigh?"

"No. I recently moved my belongings out of the apartment that Tyler and I shared. Nolan and I cleaned it out a few days ago. I reached under the bed to hide things that I wasn't bringing to Nolan's at that moment, and I found the gun."

"What did you do with the gun after you found it?" Officer Hilling asks.

"I yelled for…" I start to speak before Nolan interrupts me.

"Well, since Tyler is already violent enough, I instructed Aliza not to touch it. I unloaded it and brought it home with us. I am almost positive it would be a threat to

Aliza, and anyone else who he felt played a part in Liza leaving him.

"I did plan on calling my one friend to pick it up, since he's an officer, too. I just haven't had time to do that yet. There has been a lot going on with that asshole, Officer. She left him due to the abuse, nothing more and nothing less. I couldn't risk Aliza's life, or anyone else's, by leaving that gun there."

"Can you give me the details about this weapon, and do you know if it's registered in Mr. Smith's name or if he has a permit to carry?" Officer Hilling asks, continuing to jot our every word.

"Honestly, I don't think he has it registered in his name. He might, but I know he doesn't have a permit to carry, or he wouldn't have hid it under our bed. It's a 9 millimeter, a Ruger. At least, that's what Nolan tells me. I never saw it until the other night and tonight, when he came to Nolan's, that was the first thing he wanted. I don't know if he took the gun out of Nolan's house or what happened," I tell the officers.

"Listen, I just sent my friend to go check my house to see if the gun is still there," Nolan says.

"Okay, well here's the thing – you need to call your friend and tell him to leave the house, if he is there. Also, tell him not to touch anything and if he isn't there yet, tell him not to worry about it. Officer Michaels is radioing in a notice to set a crime scene up, if they haven't already. We would like to know if you can allow us in your house to see if the gun is there or not. Listen, we won't enter without you there, Mr. Jackson. And at this point, we don't care what else you have in there. Our main concern is getting that gun out of Mr. Smith's hands and off the street," the officer says.

Nolan stands up and grabs his phone. "I'll call Shawn now and go smoke. I'll be right back. Are you okay, Liza, or do you want me to stay in here? I will if you want me to. If you need me."

I shake my head no and he leans over to give me a kiss.

The officers continue their questions.

"Aliza, can you give us a description of Mr. Smith? If he knocked you unconscious, chances are he got into the house. Right now, we will treat this as if he took the gun. In situations like this, where a weapon might be involved, we need to consider him armed and dangerous until we can prove otherwise."

"Tyler is about six feet tall, with blonde hair. He has a few tattoos. One on his back, some on his leg and on his hand. He has green eyes and a skinny build. Officer, I can't even tell you where he could be. I don't know much about his friends or even him anymore. He has no job, no car and basically no home, since I changed the locks on my apartment. I am in the middle of moving out by the first of the month. Here's his phone number. Things weren't as bad as this. It never resulted with me going to the emergency room, though." I start crying, again.

Officer Hilling finishes up writing, looks up and sternly says, "Listen, I'm going to get this filed and Officer Michaels and I will take action to pursue him. Then we can file charges on him, immediately."

The door opens slowly and Nolan walks in. He doesn't sit down; instead, he walks up to the officers and tells them that Shawn didn't get to his house yet and that he won't go there. As Nolan and the officers talk, their voices all seem to fade away. I shut my eyes and lay there quietly. I don't think much about anything other than going home.

Considering what took place tonight, you would assume that I had a lot on my mind. I mean, any normal person would probably be replaying the incident in their head over and over. Me, on the other hand, I desensitize myself from Tyler's abuse. Granted, this was the worse he had ever lost control. After about ten minutes, Nolan's voice is growing louder, as I came back into consciousness with it.

"Aliza, I called your mother and your sister. I told them you're being discharged shortly and they can come over as soon as we get home. I figured you didn't want anyone else to bother you in here – that's why I told them the doctor suggested fewer visitors," Nolan informs me.

The policemen walk over to my bedside while Officer Michaels begins to speak. "Miss Leigh, you did a very brave thing by telling us the truth. You would be amazed by how many people in your place with injuries that are far more excessive don't want to put their abusers in jail for reasons that we could never understand because we aren't in their shoes. Know that you are one person out of more than one million who are abused every year in this country. Sadly, most people are too afraid to report the abuse to the police.

"You should be very proud of yourself tonight, despite having to endure this horrible situation. Miss Leigh, your courage was the right step to protect yourself. Maybe another person in the future, too. As an officer, I think it would be in your best interest to file a Protection from Abuse Order against Mr. Smith," Officer Michaels lectures.

Officer Michaels is right. Filing the order will ensure that I'll never have to go through this again. Hopefully Tyler doesn't do this to another woman like the scum he is. He swears he has all the power and strength, but he's wrong! He has *nothing*. For the first time in years, I realize that I'm the one with the power and strength. I always had this power and strength within, and that's why he tried to control me. My power has always been a threat to him... it scared him and it angered him to know that I was stronger than him, so he physically, mentally, emotionally and sexually tried to tear me down with his abuse, intentionally trying to destroy me.

He didn't destroy anything, though – he did the opposite. He made me even more powerful and gave me more courage, because at the end of the day I took control over this situation and I put his abuse to an end. I am the one who did the destroying for the right reasons, unlike him.

I throw my legs over the side of the bed and sit up. "Officer, I want to file the PFA, actually. Can I do that? Oh, and I forgot until now, I think he stole my purse. I had it when I was leaving, then I put my keys in it... only seconds before I noticed him. I don't see it here, and when I woke up I asked Nolan about it, but he said I was alone on the porch. I think Tyler grabbed my purse to get the keys. I know he got into the house, especially since he was there to get the gun back in the first place," I explain to Officer Hilling.

"What I can do is file for a temporary PFA, due to the injuries you obtained and for the fact that he possibly has a deadly weapon. However, you will have to show up to a hearing to put the order into permanent effect. We are going to charge him with assault to the third degree, harassment, stalking, trespassing and, if he did steal your purse, he will be charged with a petty theft crime. In addition to those charges, if we find out that he did indeed get into Mr. Jackson's house, he will be facing charges for breaking and entering.

"If we find him with the gun and it's not registered in his name, then he will have a whole string of charges for that, alone. We don't play games when it comes to domestic abuse.

"What are the best numbers to reach you at? Officer Michaels and I will contact you both when we find him. Also, we will have an officer parked by your residence in the meantime, this way the officer can walk into the house with you, when they discharge Aliza. By law, we are required to access the crime scene before there is room to tamper with any evidence. Obviously, neither I nor Officer Michaels is worried about you tampering with anything, but having prior knowledge of the gun means we have to follow protocol. It's crucial that we figure out if he was able to gain access to that gun. Also, here is my card and Officer Michaels' card. Don't worry, Mr. Smith won't be on the streets for long," he reassures Nolan and I.

"Please call my number first and if I don't answer, feel free to call Nolan. Thank you for your help, I really appreciate it," I whisper as loudly as I can.

"Thank you, officers, we appreciate everything," Nolan says while shaking each of their hands.

"You're welcome," they say in unison.

Officer Hilling continues, "We will contact you as soon as something changes. Officer Michaels and I will start the search once we walk out of this hospital. Good luck and keep her safe, Mr. Jackson. We will be in touch."

The second the door shuts behind them, I lose it again. I can't understand why I'm the one who was handed this card in life. I cover my face and just sit there crying like a helpless infant. From talking to the officers to bawling like this, my whole head is killing me. I can't recall feeling pain this bad, ever.

"Why did this happen to me? Am I that terrible of a person, did I deserve what Tyler dished out over the last few years? WHAT THE HELL?!" I try to yelled, but I can barely open my mouth enough to do so.

"Aliza, listen to me! You didn't, and don't, deserve any of the things that Tyler did. The only shitty person in this situation is that asshole, okay? It's not your fault, you were fooled by a good actor. A liar. A manipulator. I have never met a better person than you. You're always going above and beyond for the people you care about, and you have given people your last dollar if they needed it. I don't know why you had to go through this, but what I do know is you went through it and it's over.

"Do you hear me? You will NEVER go through this, AGAIN. I will NEVER put my hands on you to hurt you, and neither will he. He screwed up big-time. He has no idea the karma that he's going to face during his life! Bad people do things to good people, for whatever awful reason. You are a threat to him. He is a goddamn coward and will NEVER be able to hold the title of a good man," Nolan preaches, as he sits down beside me and holds my head in his hands.

I pull his hands down from my beat-up face, throw his arms around me and fall into him. I need him to just carry my weight, if for only for a moment. My body was limp, but now my mind won't stop racing. All I want to do is put my life on pause. The second I close my eyes, all I can see are flashbacks of Tyler gripping and screaming in my face. Then, him actually laughing with me when it was a good day, cuddling with me on his parents' pool deck during cool summer nights. But then, the next stream of memories is images of him hitting me in the face or smashing things around the house. Our relationship was twenty percent good, thirty percent denial and fifty percent terrible and toxic. Tyler was poison… deadly poison. A poison that depleted me of all the joy, love and confidence that I had. A poison that clouded my mind and believe me, it had the full potential to turn my heart into ice…I feared I would never be myself again all due to one selfish, narcissistic person. However, the poison doesn't last forever, and although survivors of abuse will never be the same, you will be nearly indestructible in many ways.

When the nurse comes in with the discharge papers, I don't say a word. I nod my head, sign the release and listen to her instructions on what to do regarding my care. The second she leaves the room, I don't waste any time getting up. I want to go home… now. Luckily, I have Nolan to help me get dressed, since I am unbelievably sore. I don't recall ever feeling this pained after a fight with that scum.

"When we get home, you should lay down. I'll handle the cops and the gun thing. I just want you to chill out and take a break. When the cops leave, I'll run you a bath, if you aren't sleeping… ya got me?" he says, while trying to get us home, faster than usual.

"Thank you. I would love to lay down and sleep for the next three days, if I could. I'm worn out. Can you call my supervisor, explain what happened and request that five PTO days be used? Tyler has no heart, no remorse or anything. I almost feel like the only joy he gets is the simple fact that he is responsible for hurting others."

Nolan doesn't say a word. I don't think he knows what to say. Nobody would know what to say, unless they are going through this kind of thing or went through it, and I get it. The silence at this moment is nice, considering I haven't had silence since the second that I woke up. I have to admit, knowing how hard Nol is trying to protect me makes me appreciate him more than I ever have. Protection isn't something I've had before from a significant other.

CHAPTER 18

Nolan hasn't even helped me out of the car completely before we notice two officers standing at the bottom of the porch steps. There is no way I'm going to be able to relax with these cops rummaging through the house. This is going to be a long night; I can already tell. One

"Miss Leigh – hi, I'm Officer Daine. Officer Hilling and Officer Michaels radioed myself and my partner Officer Tomaski in to sweep the interior of Mr. Jackson's house for the handgun. We would really appreciate it if you could bring us directly to the spot where the gun was. Just as I'm sure you two want, we want to be in and out of here, too." He looks at Nolan.

Often times I hear people making comments about cops having a love for donuts and coffee, over abundantly. Our officers in Middtown must have missed that part of the job overview, though! Similar to Officer Hilling, Officer Tomaski is very tall and husky. He has bright blue eyes and jet-black hair, carefully parted to the left side and slicked back. Tomaski is a lot younger than Officer Hilling and his muscles are perfectly sculpted from what's visible. Officer Michaels seems like he is new to the squad because he aimlessly follow Officer Daine around. He looked like he and Officer Daine were related, half-brothers, possibly. The green eyes they both had and similar shades of brown hair was uncanny. Officer Daine looked to be youngest out of all of them, though.

"No problem. You can follow me." Nolan takes the lead while helping me into the house.

I kick off my shoes and sit on the couch. Nolan can handle this, particularly because I really don't know where he hid the gun. I grab my phone and text my mom, telling her that we are home, but there are police here. I tell her that she, Alora and my dad can come over in a little bit and that I'll call them when these cops leave. The cops who took my statement weren't that intimidating; they were super nice and explained everything to me. This officer whatever-his-name-is seems like he needs some more work in the communication part of his career. He hasn't said anything and neither has his partner, at least not that I can hear.

All of a sudden, both officers are running down the steps with Nolan trailing close behind.

"What the hell is going on?" I'm asking anyone at this point.

"Miss Leigh, I'm not trying to cut you short here, but we need you and Mr. Jackson to stay close to your phones. Officer Hilling has just radioed us to leave the premises to aid in the arrest of Mr. Smith."

"Does that mean they caught him?"

Officer Daine continues out the door. "I won't know the details until I get there. We are ordered to stick to one radio frequency, which means I can't say too much at this point. Stay by the phones and someone will contact you, as soon as possible."

During our time with these officers, it is apparent that Officer Daine is more laid-back than the cops we have encountered. It also isn't hard to tell that he doesn't fit in amongst the others as effortlessly. I know age gaps among adults always make it hard for our generation. We are known as the crybaby millennials in this world, which could be why he didn't seem to fit in as much. Yet the second there was a possibility of escalation within this situation, both officers seamlessly bonded together with one common goal.

"AGH! Why won't they tell me anything?" I ask Nolan in frustration.

Nolan and I saw the officers out, watching them get in their cars. While they quickly drive off with their sirens wailing, my stomach is suddenly in knots.

"I have no idea, but the gun isn't here. That scumbag has no idea what is coming his way. It look like he may have himself jammed up now… In the meantime, you shouldn't worry about anything. Come upstairs, while I run your bath."

I pick my phone up from the table and follow Nolan to the bathroom. I am way too tired for this drama tonight. It's late, my head hurts and I just want to be in bed, asleep. I need to shut my mind off, give my emotions a little break and move on from this.

Bringing in some towels and washcloths, Nolan shuts the water off and helps me into the tub. "Give me a yell if you need anything, okay?" he says, while slowly closing the door.

This bath is probably the closest thing to heaven right now. The hot water instantly soothed the aches and pains, and I actually feel relaxed.

"Will I ever get a break tonight?" I ask myself out loud as I hear my phone. Of course, I shouldn't be mad that my mother is calling, considering she did just get news that her daughter was in the hospital with a concussion caused by her ex-boyfriend.

"Hi, Mom."

"Oh my God, are you okay?! What the hell happened? Aliza, we all went into shock when Nolan called us and told us that you were in the hospital. You better have pressed charges on that lowlife! This has gotten way out of control, and it breaks my heart and the rest of the family's to see you go through this," she yells.

"Listen, it's over with. I'm okay, nothing major here. I just have a bump on my head and I'm kind of sore. I honestly cannot be lectured right now, Mom. I gave the police a statement and they are going to railroad him with charges, all of which he deserves."

I can hear my dad saying something in the background, but I can't make out what he is telling her. "What's Dad saying?"

"Your father wants to know if you want to stay here at our house until they make an arrest. What is going on with you and Nolan? Your sister said you are moving out of your apartment?"

"No, I'm fine here…Nolan isn't going to leave this house without me, until Tyler is caught. The apartment is all cleared out, I just have to clean a little bit and do some touch-ups. Nolan and Shawn changed the locks, so Tyler cannot get in there. Plus,

Jennifer told me that he isn't welcome on premises either.

"I'm sorry I haven't told you and Dad about all the things going on, but it has been very hectic and overwhelming. Now, I just want to get this disaster behind me, in order to move on with my life," I explain, nearly in tears.

My mom lets out a sigh. "We understand, honey. We just wish you would have told us what was going on. Then we could have done something to help prevent this. Overall, your Dad and I are just grateful that tonight didn't end up any worse than it already is. We'll let you rest tonight, but we will come over tomorrow. Please, call us if you need anything – I don't care what time it is. I'll bring the phone upstairs with me, in case you call.

"Let Nolan know that we are thankful for everything he has done and is continuing to do for you. This isn't an easy situation for a young woman. However, you are handling it well. Your dad does want you to get in touch with a lawyer this week, more like first thing tomorrow. He said he can get some recommendations first. Will that be better for you?"

"Yeah, thanks. Ask him if he can please do that for me and call me with some names tomorrow or whenever. I don't know if they got Tyler yet or what is going to happen, but when he is arrested, he's screwed. I'll talk to you guys tomorrow, but I need to go to sleep. Love you guys, thanks."

"We love you too, goodnight! Please call us first thing in the morning. I'll bring something up for you guys, then you won't have to cook anything."

"Wait... Mom... hello?"

"What's wrong?" she asks, quickly.

"Can you call my job tomorrow and tell them I need the rest of the week off? Let them know that someone will drop my hospital papers off tomorrow sometime. Tell them I want to use my paid time for these days, please. I would call, but I want to sleep in, if I could, and I don't want to burden Nolan with it. Is that okay? If you can call, please do it at like seven o'clock in the morning."

"No problem, I'll take care of that for you. Go relax. Love you!"

"Thanks... okay, love you, too," I reply.

I hop out of the tub, brush my teeth in a half-assed way and powerwalk the best I can into the bedroom. The second I lay on the bed, I finally feel better.

"You okay?" Nolan asks.

"I am now, since I'm in our bed and not a hospital bed."

"Good, then move over and let me join you," he says, all the while crawling under the blankets.

"My mom called. Everyone is coming over tomorrow, and my dad is going to research some lawyers. She was a nervous wreck, and I doubt she will be sleeping much tonight. I feel bad about worrying them so much. I kind of want to turn my phone on silent, but the cops didn't call us, which I'm assuming that means nothing good, right?" I ask.

"I don't know. Do you want me to call one of them? I have their cards in my wallet."

I sit up and gave him a quiet yes, nodding my head. He gets out of bed, walks across the room, grabs his wallet and crawls back under the blankets. He lights a cigarette and proceeds to call one of the officers from the emergency room.

"Hi, this is Nolan Jackson. I'm calling on behalf of Aliza Leigh. Earlier we had two cops at my residence looking for the gun, which isn't here. Anyway, during that time, they left in a hurry and said they needed to pursue and apprehend Tyler Smith. Was he arrested?" Nolan questions the officer who answered the phone stating his name as Officer Creeger.

All I hear is a bunch of jumbled words from the other end, and Nolan saying vague replies like, "oh okay" and "then what happened". Obviously Tyler wasn't arrested – at least, it doesn't sound like that. After a few minutes of more nebulous replies and some hand gestures, it becomes clear that they didn't arrest him. Now, I'm aggravated.

"Well...?" I look at Nolan for answers.

"He's still on the streets. They thought they had him, but it wasn't Tyler. That means they are back to square one. On the other hand, they have an officer on standby in front of our house, since they have to assume Tyler is 'armed and dangerous', considering he said his motive for coming here was to take his gun."

I shake my head in disgust, "Great... that makes me feel better, NOT," I say, sarcastically.

"Go to bed. This is the safest place for you right now, especially since you basically have guards outside the house. You know he won't come here when I'm home – he only shows up when I leave."

"You're right. I need sleep, anyway."

"I agree. Did you call work, or do you want me to call your job in the morning?" he asks.

"No, my mom said she will handle that for me. Actually, can you drop off my excuse tomorrow? My parents and my sister are coming to visit for a bit, maybe you can sneak out when they get here and get that done."

He reaches over and shuts the light off. "Not a problem. I want to run to the store, anyway. We need some stuff to eat and drink." Finally, we're on the same page about that.

Entry #80

It's been a long minute since we have last spoken. Tyler landed me in the hospital, I'm out of work for a damn week and he is still on the run! Nolan refuses to leave the house without me, too. My family and Ally stopped over today and all I heard was my mother cry and complain about what happened, like I don't know how awful he is. Oh, and good news, my dad found a lawyer. Mr. Lawyer was highly recommended by a handful of people, plus he specializes in cases like this. I feel good about Tyler getting exactly what he deserves!

I've decided to stay off social media for the upcoming weeks, or at least until this disaster blows over. I know Tyler's parents will try to make a mockery of me, most likely claiming that I exaggerated this whole ordeal. Tyler being arrested will cause a lot of animosity towards me, especially from his parents. Unfortunately, social media will be their biggest outlet. Dealing with this is hard enough; I don't need to read their slander about me. My phone hasn't stopped ringing because everyone wants to wish me well or ask me what happened. It's easy to tell who is legitimately concerned, and who is being nosy.

I'm exhausted. My whole visit with my family was a blur, but I am happy they came to visit me and Nolan. My doctor ordered me painkillers to help with the bruises, but I couldn't take them until I was out of the concussion zone. I may or may not have taken a little more than I should have, but that's beside the point. Still no word on Tyler – he's on the run and it's a nightmare. I would like to wish him the best in life, but I feel bitter right now. ~~I missed you... did you miss me?~~ I missed writing in this notebook. There, that sounds way better and not as crazy. I need sleep and <u>no visitors</u>. I can't help but love his persistence and dedication to keeping me safe. I'm not used to my boyfriend being a good man.

Sincerely,

The girl who needs a new start, starting with a new journal

I close my journal and throw it in my bag. The television is on in the living room and I'm sure Nolan thinks that I'm asleep, which is fine. He needs to relax, anyway. I grabbed my cell phone, start to type and sent a copy-and-pasted text to my mother, father, my sister and Jen the landlord.

"Thanks for coming over today! I feel bad that I was so tired and just feeling blah, but these meds definitely make me want to sleep! I'll call tomorrow. I'm going to bed... again lol. Goodnight!"

Before I know it, my sister replies with multiple texts.

"Np, get some rest bc you know this is just the beginning of the chaos."

"I hope you're not mad that I told mom & dad about you and Nolan dating. I figured everything would make more sense if they knew before coming over."

"It's okay. I should have told them but it's been hectic. They seemed relieved... kinda confused, but I think it was a lot to take in @ the moment. I wonder if Nolan is going to tell his parents. IDT he has talked to either of them in a month."

The moment I begin to fall asleep, I heard my phone notify me of yet another text from Alora.

"They always had a weird family dynamic behind closed doors. I told mom not to say anything bc that wasn't the time or place. They're ok w/ it but you know mom will say something eventually."

I can't find the energy to reply. I'm worn out, physically sore and, if it wasn't for the cops telling us to pay attention to my phone, the device would be powered down by now. I should call Nol and find out what time he is coming upstairs, but he has been waiting on me hand and foot. I never thought that I would get involved in a relationship that feels normal, for the most part. Well, there's no such thing as normal, but after dealing with dysfunction, this feels very normal to me. As I'm drifting into sleep, I can hear the text alerts on my phone. I'm way too exhausted to even look at the screen. I'm positive those texts won't disappear any time between now and when I wake up.

CHAPTER 19

"Aliza… Babe… hey, you need to wake up for a minute."

I pull the blanket over my head and swat Nolan away. There is no reason for him to wake me, considering I don't have work today or tomorrow. All I have to do is file the papers for the PFA, which can be done at any time before four o'clock.

"Aliza you NEED to wake up!" he says while shaking my arm gently.

"I don't *have* to wake up. Go back to sleep. I'll wake up in a little bit!" I yell at him.

"Oh my god", I yell at the empty room as my phone continues going off.

"Aliza, Tyler's been calling you nonstop. He's been texting and calling you since two in the morning, apparently," Nolan informs me.

"Why? Does he not realize he is wanted because he can't keep his hands to himself? I know he's stupid – he can't be that stupid, though! Will you just answer it for me? I don't want to talk to him."

Nolan reaches over me to get my phone as I force myself upright. He puts it on speaker, so I can hear the whole conversation.

"Yo. It's after three in the morning. Stop calling Aliza. Did you forget that you're on the run for physically assaulting her or what?" he screams into the phone.

"Lies, lies and more lies. Your girlfriend, who I had first, *let* me into your house! Such a great girlfriend she is, right?" Tyler laughs.

I ripped the phone out of Nolan's hand. "Don't start this shit. I NEVER let you in! Nolan and I were together before he left. He knows I didn't call you over! Did I bruise myself, too? You need to turn yourself in and leave me alone! Today you will be served with PFA papers, by the way, whenever they find where you're hiding. Right now I have a temporary PFA against you! I'm calling the cops too! You have been calling me for the last hour, oh, and sending me text after text. YOU ARE DONE! You are going to jail! Tyler, you are finally going to get hit… with karma! It's karma for everything you have ever done to me and everyone else in your life," I yell.

"If I'm going to jail, I'm going to jail for something worth it! CALL THE COPS! Call the cops and tell them… t-tell them that I'm waiting for them now! Let them know my 9 millimeter is right here. Tell them to come and find me! Ya better give them a heads-up because I prom… promise you one of us won't be walking out of here alive. Let that sink in. Let that rest on your conscience," he slurs, stuttering.

"Aliza, hang the phone up," Nolan orders.

"Oh, does it bother you that your new girlfriend is talking to m*e*?" Tyler mocks in a childlike tone.

"I. AM. DONE. You will not threaten me with something like that. Nothing I do to you will ever rest on my conscience like what you did to me. I don't know what you're on right now, but you're acting like a fucking lunatic, and you are going to get yourself killed. This isn't a game!"

Nolan grabs the phone. "You call Aliza's phone again and I will personally get in my car and come beat your ass…" Nolan hangs up.

He hands me the phone and pulls me close to him. I feel like I want to cry my eyes out, but I am sick of being Tyler's victim. I am not a victim, I am a survivor. We sit there in silence until my phone starts to ring again.

"I'm not answering it," I say while hitting the decline button. When the call ends, I unlock my phone and dial 9-1-1. I don't hesitate or think about any other ways to handle this. It will never stop if I don't do this, and I know that.

As the call connects, my palms get sweaty and my stomach is in knots. "What's your emergency?" the dispatcher asks.

"Hi. I currently have a temporary PFA against my abusive ex-boyfriend. He physically attacked me, which resulted in hospitalization. He's currently on the run from the police, due to charges pressed after the incident. He won't stop calling me or threatening me."

"Can I have his name and address, please?" she asks.

"His name is Tyler Smith. I have no idea where he is – he won't tell me – but he does have a loaded gun on him, or so he claims."

"Okay, can I please have your name and address? I am sending an officer out to speak to you and get the information in order to pursue Mr. Smith?"

I give her all the information she needs and hang up. If I wasn't so tired, I would count the number of times Tyler has called and texted me. I'm estimating, well, over thirty at least!

"Can you light me a cigarette?" I ask Nolan.

"Of course. Aliza, I really don't like him doing all this psychotic shit. I didn't know he was this bad. I knew your arguments turned physical… I didn't think he was this out of his mind, though. It's almost like he is two people living in one body. Does he take medications or anything?"

I grab the cigarette and crawl next to him. "He won't take any medications. I don't know why he thinks the psychologist and psychiatrist are out to make his life worse. Obviously they are doing their jobs the correct way, but he is just so backwards and it makes him think people purposely mess with him to make him mad or something…

"It's screwed up and possibly the worst kind of paranoia I have ever witnessed. There will never be a chance for him because he is so far gone. He fluctuates from one extreme to the next, which makes everything ten times crazier. That asshole will put his hands on me, but then if I get mad at him for it and start to yell or leave, then he becomes the victim and I'm the one who should apologize. I could never w-win," I say, as I feel a single tear slide down my cheek. I finally feel defeated.

Nolan scoops me up in one motion and pulls me onto his lap. He brushes my hair out of my face, then wipes away the tears from the corner of my eyes. I don't know why, but I instantly feel as if I am struck with a lightning bolt. . . a lightning bolt full of anger, regret and embarrassment. The anger stems from the fact that I have allowed Tyler to keep using me as his personal punching bag. However, the feeling of regret is the strongest emotion of them all. When you regret years, memories and just the experience of a whole person in general, that emotion trumps everything else. Then, there is good ol' embarrassment, which comes with the aftermath of abuse and having to admit you were in a relationship with such a foul, heartless, useless excuse for a man that everyone tried to save you from.

"Hold on. I'll go see who it is before you get up," Nolan says.

Clearly, he is thinking exactly what I am thinking. When I don't hear the sounds of the steps cracking and squeaking, I walk out of the bedroom and listen from the top of the staircase. Within a matter of seconds, Nolan is yelling for me to come down. For a moment, I was amazed with the officer's rapid arrival, but the realized that he had been watching the house all night.

I walk over to the front door and notice Officer Daine standing there with a female cop, one who I'm not familiar with. She is of medium height, thin with her blonde hair pulled back in a tight ballerina bun. She isn't tough-looking like the female cops you see on television shows. Surprisingly, this woman is pleasantly feminine and does her makeup in a very subtle style.

"Hi, Miss Leigh. We had a call in from dispatch. They said you called about the PFA violation and gun threats. Can you tell Officer Young and I what the situation is?"

"Well, Tyler Smith is calling me, over and over. He is telling me that he has a loaded gun. He isn't stable, as you know from the last incident and with him still on the streets. I'm terrified. He might just be talking out of his ass, but at this point I think he is crazy enough to act upon his words. I'm assuming he isn't too happy that this entire saga was reported, resulting with a warrant out for his arrest. I have no idea where he is!"

"Officer, he has called about fifty times. It's getting a little ridiculous. Actually, this whole thing is way over-the-top at this point," Nolan chimes in.

Officer Young looks up from her notepad as she writes down some things that we both said. "Officer Daine familiarized me with the situation prior to our arrival. I am going to radio in for additional assistance. We want a another car parked down the road, as well as backup aiding us in apprehending Mr. Smith, sooner than later. I'm certain that we will find him tonight. I quickly ran his name after receiving the call. I think I know who he is. Mr. Smith isn't a stranger to trouble. I am going to run out to the car and run his name again, gather his previous addresses and other data, while Officer Daine finishes up in here".

Officer Young proceeds out the door. She is all business and didn't waste time. All I want to do is puke, although I'm hoping I can hold off on that until we are done. I've had enough embarrassment and shock with all of this. What did they mean about Tyler being "no stranger" to trouble? The last thing I want to do is puke all over, though, especially while the cops are here, or even worse… puke on the cop.

"Aliza, I don't need any details about him because I have them, but I do need to know if you have any idea of his whereabouts," Officer Daine asks.

I shake my head. "I have no idea. I never know, or ever really knew, where he went when he left. I don't know who his friends are or even what he does with his time…" I say, ashamed.

"If he isn't at the addresses that you guys have for him, then what?" Nolan asks.

"In a situation like this, our best bet is probably to have Miss Leigh call his cell phone. Then we can pinpoint his location. If he is as unstable as you claim, I have no interest waiting while officers knock on doors. Baiting him is our best option."

"That makes sense, what if he is close and can see the house and all the cops here, he isn't going to answer the phone. He isn't *that* stupid. Calling him from my phone might be a little too much. He knows I wouldn't call him for just anything right now. I'm nervous that he is going to get suspicious. Can we text him from Nolan's phone… say something to get him to answer? I'm sure if I text him, acting like I'm Nolan, wanting to meet him to fight or something, he will answer," I suggest.

Officer Daine nods his head in agreement and has Nolan pull his phone out. He makes sure to inform Nolan to hold off on any real threats. I reach for the phone and begin to scroll through the contacts for Tyler's number. I don't know why I'm surprised that this is happening. Everyone has always warned me of the doom to come. Jesus, I have warned myself, too. Shaking, I find his number.

"Listen, Aliza doesn't know I'm texting you but I'm done with your shit. You won't stop

threatening her and I've had enough. Come meet me NOW bc this is being handled. IDC who gets mad or how tough you think you are."

"I sent the text. All I said was that Nolan wants to know where he can meet him. Is that okay, Officer?"

"Perfect. Now we wait. I don't think this is an instance where we will actually ping his phone."

I know that walking away from someone when they are talking, especially someone like a police officer, is rude. However, I don't care at this point. I don't care that I am dealing with this. I don't care that Officer

Daine is still talking. I don't care that Nolan is probably going to follow me and try to console me. I don't care about any of this. I don't even care that I don't care, which might not make sense. The lack of caring, in regards to something this serious, seems irresponsible and reckless, but I don't care. That has always been my problem. I care too much about everyone and everything. I've never wanted to be the cause of someone's sadness, anger or anything else.

When you get to this point in life, where do you go from here? I have no idea what I want to do with myself. I'm thankful for the support I have and the protection I have, particularly from Nol. I'm grateful that I am mostly out of this situation. The desire for Tyler to go away completely is much appreciated. Am I ever going to be that lucky? Will I have the opportunity to continue my life without fear, or without Tyler making me feel like I will never deserve happiness?

CHAPTER 20

It's going to be a long three hours. Then it happens.

"Nol, your phone is going off..."

Nolan comes running into the living room. "Here, give me the phone... What did he say?"

"I'm not sure. I don't want to look at it, honestly."

I grab my phone and dial Officer Daine's phone number. Every ring causes me to feel more overwhelmed.

"Officer Daine, what's going on?"

"Tyler answered Nolan. What do we do now?"

Calmly he says, "Nothing. Nobody reply until I get there. I haven't had any luck with his parents. They refuse to give me any information about his whereabouts. At this point, we are starting the process of obtaining a search warrant. I'll be over with another officer shortly."

"Okay, I'll let Nolan know." I hang the phone up and stand there like I am frozen for a minute. I have no idea what is going to happen, but for once I almost feel content.

Before I can turn the corner, Nolan walks into the kitchen. "What did he say?"

"Nothing, really. Don't answer the text until Daine gets here."

"Sounds easy enough. I think Tyler might be drunk or something, his whole attitude changed. He wrote, *"Good luck trying to railroad me with Aliza. It's like she has been waiting for the perfect moment to screw me over. She leaves me for you, and now she wants to put me in jail. I'm NOT going to jail, though. You can come to me. I'm not falling into your trap to be locked up. It's not going down that way. I have a good idea of what charges I'm getting hit with and the time they hold."*

I look at Nolan, puzzled. Not at the fact of blame being put on me, but because Ty's attitude did change somehow.

"What happens..." But before I can finish my sentence, there is a knock on the door.

"I'll get it, relax. It's going to be okay."

I follow Nolan's directions.

Nolan and Officer Daine are talking with one another. I can't make out what they are saying. Not that I'm really trying that hard to figure it out, either.

"Miss Leigh, I'm going to have you and Nolan text him back. Simply ask where he is and agree to meet him. I am going to let you know ahead of time – right now he's armed and dangerous. I don't want to scare you, but we don't approach this kind of situation lightly. There will be backup… a lot of backup. None of us like to deal with situations like this, so let's all pray it goes well. Criminal or not, we do not want anyone to be hurt or in danger."

No words come out. I shake my head in agreement and silently sit there. Nolan follows Officer Daine's directions, due to my incompetent state. My family has no idea what is going on right now, and I have no energy to bother them with this crazy bullshit.

I hear the phone go off almost instantly, like Tyler has been anticipating Nolan's reply.

"1674 Staton Avenue… it's the condemned house with tan shutters."

"That's all he said," Nolan confirms.

"Are you going there now?" I ask the officer.

He puts his radio back on his belt. "Yes, and I will let you know when he is apprehended. Don't worry, Miss Leigh, everything is going to be okay. Sometimes the ending isn't always the easiest. You are doing the right thing."

Nolan walks over and wraps me up in a tight hug. "If you didn't do this, you would have gone through hell for your whole life. Living in fear for your safety. I'm positive of that."

"I know. Why am I worried about being the bad guy? Is that selfish of me?"

"Not at all," he says, kissing my forehead. "Let's go lay down on the couch. I'd say we have a long night ahead of us, but the night's long gone. Better yet, you lay down and I'll make us some breakfast."

"Can you just stay with me for a minute? I just need you to lay with me."

Nolan gives me a smile and bows his head. The smile is full of pity, as if he can't say no to me without it resulting in guilt. At this point I'll take the pity *and* a cigarette.

"Babe, you really are way stronger than you give yourself credit for. All this time you've been dealing with the craziest shit. You have never acted like it was this bad or hinted that your life was this tumultuous. I'm sorry. I should have paid more attention," Nolan says, his voice overflowing with sadness. I curl up against him. "Don't apologize. You have always been here for me, thank you."

"Are you hungry or anything?"

"No, I'm not sure I can really eat right now. Hey, do you think I should call my mom?"

He pulls his phone out, but dials my sister's number. I grab it and let it ring until the voicemail picks up. I then pull my mother's number up and let that ring. She doesn't answer, either.

"Alora didn't answer, and neither did my mother," I say. Maybe they will answer if I call them from my cell phone. The problem is, I don't know where I put my phone.

As I get up to look for it, all of a sudden I hear banging on the door... we both look at each other in a panic. "Liza, go sit down. Officer Daine said he would call. This doesn't sound like Officer Daine. I don't know who this is."

The second Nolan answers the door, my sister and my mother come barreling through.

"What are …"

"Turn the news on now! We have been trying to call your phone!" my mom yells.

"We couldn't remember Nolan's phone number and with everything going on we got scared!" Alora cries.

"What's going on with you guys? I mean, the cops were here. Everyth—"

My mom cuts me off. "We actually came here to tell you there's a hostage situation."

"Wait… Tyler?!", I questioned nervously.

Remaining calm, "Mom, what is going on? What do you mean, hostage situation?"

Nolan runs and grabs the remote, planning to put the news on, but is fumbling with the device. I don't know if he is in a state of shock or nervous like I am. In spite of what is happening right now, we all were friends once… for the most part.

Nolan walks over and put his hand on my right leg. "What is he doing now?", I asked

Nolan, not that he knew anything more than the rest of us.

We all sit in silence, listening to the news reporter.

"Rachelle Nollson, reporting from a location on Staton Avenue. At the moment, all we know is that local police are in the process of an apprehension. From what we were able to gather, a man by the name of Tyler Smith is currently holding himself hostage. There has been no comment from the officers yet, considering we can't get close. As soon as we have an update..."

Then I hear it. I hear it before she even finishes her sentence.

I hear one shot…

Then I hear my mom gasp, my sister gasp and Nolan gasp, all in unison.

Nobody says a word for what seems like an eternity.

"Rachelle Nollson, reporting at the hostage location. We have now learned that there was a single gunshot. We can confirm that it came from inside the condemned property. However, we are not sure if anyone is present with Mr. Smith. We will have more information, when we return."

"This is my fault. This is all my fault!!" I cry out.

Before I can hit the floor, Nolan catches me. I can't believe Ty did this.

My mom stands up and hugs me. "*You* didn't do anything wrong. This could have been you. Or Nolan...or anybody at all. You could have been ki—" she starts to cry. Not just a normal cry, it's a painful cry, her body heaving with sobs. A cry that only a mother can cry, outpouring her fear and protective nature, as she keeps squeezing me tighter and tighter.

Nolan's phone is ringing, but he can't let go of me, either. I look up at my sister and she immediately answers it for us.

Although the three of us can only hear Alora's responses, it is pretty obvious that Office Daine has confirmed exactly what we already knew.

"Aliza..." my sister hands me the phone.

"Hello?" I say, barely able to hold the device.

"Miss Leigh, I know this chain of events hasn't been the easiest for you, and I'm sure you have heard the news already. When we arrived at the location Mr. Smith was not wanting to come out, before pursuing him, we tried to engage with him from the outside. We have certain orders that must be followed when someone is suspected to be armed and dangerous. Mr. Smith was not cooperating, while verbally threating us and showing his weapon.

"We radioed in more officers and medical personnel, in case he opened fire during that time. We were unable to coax him out of the house safely before he pulled the trigger on himself. Mr. Smith died of a self-inflicted wound to the head," Office Daine slowly confirms.

"I caused this," I whisper, horrified.

I hear the officer take a deep breath. "You didn't cause this. It's a tragedy all within itself, but I had a feeling this was going to happen. Whether it was now, like this, or twenty-five years from now and God forbid, he did this to you or anyone else for that matter. Sometimes a person is able to see the hurt they cause others, but they aren't sure how to stop themselves from causing that hurt. If it's because they don't receive the right kind of help or for another reason, I have no idea. All I know is you can't help everyone and you can't prevent things from happening. You can only help yourself, and that's what you did. Protecting yourself, that's the bravest thing a person can do," Officer Daine says quietly.

I don't say a word back to the officer. I hand the phone to Nolan and I stand there for a minute. My mother comes over to hug me, then my sister follows. They cry, but I'm not sure what they are crying for, exactly. I know a lot of those tears are for me, rather than Tyler, and I understand. I hug them both back, tighter than I ever have before.

Nolan is still on the phone with Officer Daine. He walks over, gives me a kiss on my forehead, and softly tells me he will be off in a minute. He is in shock; I know he is. All of us are shocked. He gently pushes me against his chest, and I feel a weird sensation of simultaneous peace and guilt. I let go and walk up the steps. I stand against the vanity. I am not positive I would have been standing much, if it isn't for the furniture holding me up. I inhale the stale air and exhale slowly. Tonight, my reflection isn't so filtered. I guess I feel admiration for the unfiltered and broken side of who I am. The real me, the damned me, the beautifully mended, the flawed me. I feel an overwhelming deal of sadness, guilt and uncertainty that came with all of this.

A situation like this will never be fully processed, since I don't know how to understand it being reality. I never imagined it ending this way. I imagined it ending differently, incredibly differently. But I feel unexpected relief. I feel free, and that is exactly why the guilt has set in. It's almost like these imaginary chains that I have worn for all those years are now gone. The chains that have held me back from happiness, the chains that have weighed me down every day; chains that have kept me tied to someone who loved me the wrong way, a dangerous way.

I always thought of myself as Tyler's biggest victim. That claim is undeniably accurate in many, many ways. Nevertheless, tonight I realized that Tyler's biggest victim was, always himself. Because of that, I hope he can feel free and relieved that he isn't wearing the chains he forged for himself any longer. These heavy chains have done more damage to him than they have ever done to me. I understand that sometimes our ending is dictated by different things and sometimes we can't control the outcome. After everything I have went through, I want a different ending, a better ending than this.

Amanda Burke Jaworski is a twenty-seven-year-old mother of two children, Alexa and Jojo. She currently resides in Scranton, Pennsylvania with her daughter, son, and their father. Let's not forget their two dogs, Bandit and Raven! Beside writing and publishing her work, she is a nurse's aide and graphic designer. She also possesses an associate degree in Early Childhood Education and Development.  When she isn't busy with her very incredible children or one of the above roles mentioned, you can find her lost in a novel, quad riding, exploring the great outdoors or enjoying time with family and friends. She loves laughing, astrology, photography and experiencing anything new, all with the intention of having fun during this lifetime and building new memories.

For more information on the author, future titles, or additional merchandise, find us on the web at

amandabjaworski.com

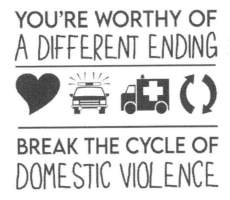

Made in the USA
Middletown, DE
30 September 2020